THE NURSE-KEEPER

Nanette Ackerman

First Published in 2021 by Blossom Spring
Publishing
The Nurse-Keeper Copyright © 2021

Nanette Ackerman

ISBN 978-1-8382421-9-0

E: admin@blossomspringpublishing.com

W: www.blossomspringpublishing.com

To George

2020

In 17th Century England the River Thames was alive with commerce. Ships from far across the world sailed into port disgorging their cargoes onto the quay to be loaded onto carts. Mariners from far off lands, sweating with toil, filled taverns and tankards alike, while the merchants tallied their goods.

In 1660, the bells of old London Town rang out the return of King Charles II to the English throne. Thousands of citizens thronged the streets in jubilation to welcome back their Monarch. Flags and ribbons flying in a victorious parade of colourful pageantry put an end to the gloomy age of Commonwealth. Soon, theatres were built and re-opened, actors dusted down their Shakespeare and women cavorted on the stage. Gaming houses and taverns spun with coin once more, and it is not hard to imagine that, after eighteen years of suppression, lewd laughter again reverberated from these iniquitous establishments, attracting the censorious eyes and ears of the occasional passing Puritan, with head down, who still feared the retribution of the Lord.

By the summer of 1665, the streets of London Town were ghostly quiet. Constables patrolled the streets and, breaking curfew, people crept warily from place to place, startled by their own shadows. Hiding around corners they covered their faces clutching their kerchiefs, and mournfully the bells rang out as rumbling carts spilled over with the dead. Entire families were shut up in their houses, unable to escape the foul vapours forced upon them. Some wept and wailed, others laughed and capered – for tomorrow they might die. This was the time of the Great Plague. It is easy to look upon a collective catastrophe, numbers on the Bill of Mortality nailed to a board but these numbers represented people with hopes and fears, individuals going about their daily lives: working, idling, laughing, begging, playing. Today, we have technology, means of communication – 'systems in place' despite the inroads of a foul disease; but one thing is still as it was. In 1665, amid rampant infection, they saw the populous polarised. This was not a distinction between rich and poor, but of character. For the most part, the people of London Town, at this time, showed no redeeming feature, no flaws – just good deeds or bad and a deep void between. What is more, unexpected heroes could be found in unexpected places. This is a tragic drama – but its history is real.

In December 1664, a blazing star shot like an arrow over England. Some said that it was the brightest shooting star of all time, but for others it was a dreadful and portentous comet. There had been comets before – harbingers of drought, famine or the dreaded plague. Not long ago, down the generations in ancestral memory, was the Black Death that had swept across Europe and over the Channel to England in the 14th Century, and thousands of people had died a horrible death at the hand of a plague carried by black rats. Yet many citizens paid no heed to the omen and carried on with the comings and goings of their lives.

Imagine the springtime of 1665. In the close streets and alleyways of London Town, folk opened the windows of their little timbered houses to chatter and banter. Some tipped rubbish down into the street below, skimming the laundered linen hanging from house to house and, in the manner of a music-hall skit, perhaps caught a fellow citizen unaware. Living was rough then, insanitary, and the overhanging houses were so close that neighbours could pass tankards of ale to the folk opposite. Dogs barked and scrapped, children played, shouts and whistles hit the air. Perhaps the racket rounded the corner to the market place to catch the cries of peddlers calling their wares…

'What d' ye lack? What d' ye lack?'…

'Oranges, sweet oranges…' called the seller of fruit.

A small boy crept forward with his mouth watering

and chanced his luck. 'Oranges!'

'Cor!' said another. 'Give us an orange.'

'Nay, get thee gone ye little brats,' she answered, swinging the basket away from them.

'Just one, mistress – for all of us, just one.' He crept closer and fingered the fruit. 'There, that one, for 'tis dry as leather.'

'Nay, get thee gone, Jim Hogg!' The orange seller raised her hand to strike, but it hung in the air when a gentleman approached. 'Oh, sir, 'tis a devil to make a living with the likes of them – scrounging like dogs.'

'The likes of them?' echoed the gentleman, offering a coin.

'Well, what am I to do with Jack Hogg's little brat? He's always begging.'

'Perchance he hath need. Three oranges, if it pleases ye, mistress.'

'It pleases me, sir,' she said, 'if the coin be right.'

'Now catch!' The physician turned and threw one orange after the other: 'One two… Ah, who's that little one that doth hide behind her mother's skirts?'

A small face emerged. 'Jane, sir.'

'And one for little Jane, mistress. Now, run along home.' He turned 'Ah, James!'

'Good even, doctor. Your charges, I trust, are well?'

'Ha! Then would I be out of a job.'

'Ah, so business is good?'

The doctor shook his head and feigned regret. 'Some have the dropsy, some the falling sickness and others, 'tis sad to say, a strange ague – but the leeches do fatten. And your flock, sir? They do, I trust, likewise to thy profession, behave themselves?' he asked, removing a small flask from his pocket and swigging its contents.

The priest also shook his head and, catching sight of the doctor smacking his lips, there was irony in his tone. 'They do not, sir. A more wayward flock of sheep ne'er roamed abroad.'

'Make them into angels and ye, too, will be out of a job,' returned the doctor. 'Ye bemoan their behaviour, yet 'tis their very recalcitrance that lines thy gullet.' He laughed himself florid.

'Nay, but were there no sin,' said James with gravity, 'we would have no need for our dear Redeemer. That is the pity of it.'

'Ay, 'tis a philosophic matter.' The doctor took another swig and again smacked his lips. 'Ah, there is nothing like physic at eventide.' Then moving closer observed: 'What is that on top of thy head?'

'A head of hair, sir.'

'Nay, nay, nay. Where is thy periwig?'

'The washerwoman hath done it a mischief.'

'A mischief done to a periwig, how so?'

'A passing pigeon...'

The doctor laughed heartily.

'A plague on pigeons!' snapped the clergyman. 'Now I must purchase a new wig, for the washerwoman cleaned it with such fury that it resembles the very creature's nest.'

The doctor guffawed, his face scarlet.

The two had been friends since a child in James's congregation had begun to choke on a piece of apple on his way to church and was turning blue, whereupon the good doctor had thrust two fingers down his throat and expelled it forthwith – not before the child had pulled off the doctor's periwig in fright and it had landed in the mud to be run over by a cart. James was a serious soul, but that evening, thanks to the doctor, he had laughed and found it good medicine and told the elderly doctor he should prescribe it. They had dined together that evening and, despite James being once a Puritan and the doctor once an avid Royalist, they found that they amused each other and struck up a very unlikely friendship.

'I am ever sanguine in your company, James,' said the doctor. 'I am a member of the Royal College of Physicians – but they are choleric, James, choleric – out of humour, and one Sir Philip Hawker is the very devil. We seek not each other's company.'

'Why so?'

'I am merry, 'tis my nature to be merry – and Hawker is a callous creature. The more blood his unfortunate patients let, the more he lets blood. There is a limit to it, James, a limit.'

'Ye have a warm heart, doctor,' said the priest, 'but I hope I shall never have cause to consult Hawkins.'

'Hawker, James, Hawker. Remember his name or be damned.'

Their happy interchange was at once interrupted by the shoemaker's apprentice who appeared suddenly from the alley.

'But what...? Ah, 'tis Samuel.'

'Doctor!'

'What's afoot? Ye do not have my shoes?' He laughed loudly at his joke.

'Nay, Doctor, they are not yet made.'

'Not made? Ye did measure my feet a week hence.'

'More matter, sir. I have been looking for thee an hour since, for 'tis the bitt-maker. His 'prentice says he sickens and he knows not what to do. Some fever it is, for sure…'

'That burns his blood that would curdle in his veins before it simmers down?'

'Ay – a terrible sickness.'

'Hath he a token?'

'A token, sir?'

'A blotch, a blotch?'

'Ay, he hath. And he cries out in pain.'

'Anon I come,' said the doctor. 'God's wounds, it doth but bring a crust. Fare ye well, priest.'

'Fare ye well, my friend.'

2

It grew suddenly chilly as James turned towards St. Bride's. The sound of the local folk peddling wares began to fade with the evening light. James looked up piously as though in prayer, at once suspicious of the pigeons cooing and fluttering by the bell tower. On a sudden, one left its perch to fly to a post looking for crumbs – for there was a bakehouse selling wheaten loaves by the alley and the crumbs fell plentifully there. 'The devil!' James exclaimed, and the devil did not disappoint him. Down the muck sploshed onto his shoulder, and made a determined way down his frock coat. He grimaced and wiped it with a kerchief. First, they had ruined his excellent periwig, and now… He found an outlet for his frustration when a group of noisy children rounded the corner kicking a pig's bladder in the guise of a football. 'Halt you ruffians – calm ye down!'

'We were only playing, sir.'

'The whole of London Town is playing, sir – playing with life.'

'We do want to kick our ball!'

'Nay, 'tis nearly six-of-the-clock. Be off with ye.'

Murmurs of discontent hit the air and a boy they called Jim stepped forward. He was a smutty but honest little scrap with freckles and, finding his courage, he challenged the priest.

'We have no sins, sir.'

'No sins, no sins? What is thy name?'

'Jim Hogg, sir.'

'Ah, then I know thy father, Jack Hogg and if 'tis true

the sins of the father be visited on the children ye have the lot.'

'Nay, sir, I have none.'

'How so?'

'For that I am frightened of the constable, for he doth lock people in the stocks, sir – and in the pillory. I've seen him do it, so I do be a good boy.'

'Nay, everyone on earth hath sins, boy. Oh, and yonder stands my church, St. Bride's. If ye should care to wash thy dirty face on Sunday – and not forget thine ears – God be praised, and I shall take pains to admit thee and relieve thee of thy sins.'

'Ay, sir.' Jim bowed his head.

'Ye may go,' said James.

Jim Hogg ran off to join his friends and, kicking the bladder ball by turns, they disappeared down the alley. James smiled as he watched them go. He reckoned he'd been hard on them and it played on his conscience. He thought it good that he had a conscience and was contemplating this improvement to his soul when, looking across the way, he saw a young woman, rich in silk, watching him closely.

'Good even lady,' he said, assuming a pleasanter attitude.

'Good even, sir.'

'Ye were, perchance, venturing to the church?'

'Nay, sir, 'tis not yet Sunday.'

'My door is always open – ye may pray betimes.'

She studied him. She thought him thin of hair on top but good to look at – for a priest. Better the physical form than the man inside, she judged. 'I could not help noticing,' she continued, 'thy anger. For shame, sir, they have no sins. They are but children.'

'I was not angry. I did but seek some order in the square.'

James shifted uneasily, conscious of his unworthy appearance, for he wore no distinguished periwig, a filthy stain was evident – smudged from the shoulder down the front of his frock coat and, in this pitiful state of attire, he had evidently been thrust into the presence of a beautiful and forthright young woman.

'I own I was a little harsh,' he condescended.

'A little?' Her eyes sparkled with vitality. Yet they were unsettling, for they seemed to bore into his very soul.

'Ay, but a little.' Still uneasy, he did not return her stare, but recovering some dignity, added: 'I do not recollect thy presence at my church, lady.'

'We are newly arrived in London Town, but I shall be pointed in that direction on Sunday morning.'

'Then I shall point my sermon in your direction on Sunday morning: The sins of the fathers.'

'I cannot agree with ye sir. I have seen that little boy playing with the dogs in the alley. I did give him a penny for a wheaten loaf and he did share it with the other children – and with the pigeons.'

'He did feed the pigeons?'

'Ay, sir.'

'Then he is twice the rogue!'

'Nay. But his father is a monster. I remember Jack Hogg well, since he accosted me with his lewdness when I did arrive in Town. Did he not Peg?'

'He accosted ye?'

'With his lewdness. I dare not repeat it.'

It was then that her little maid, who had been standing at a distance swaying a basket, astonished her mistress by stepping up and whispering the in the priest's ear.

'Peg!' It was the lady's turn to be abashed.

James almost swooned in shock: 'The wretch! Did ever a more unruly ruffian stagger about in hell? The devil the plague, take him.'

'Charity, sir.'

'Ay, and I can tell thee…' continued Peg.

'Peg! What have I told thee about thy busy tongue?'

'But Madam…'

'I do apologise for my maid's indiscretion. She is young, sir, and not yet studied in propriety.'

James was satisfied that the apology had repaid a little of his dignity – until the lady's eyes alighted on his frock coat.

'What is that on thy person, sir?'

The clergyman blushed. It was distressing for a young man of the cloth to blush. 'Naught,' he replied.

'It is something,' she persisted. 'and it looks like…'

'Bird muck!' put in Peg.

'Peg!' whispered the lady, motioning for her maid to go home. 'I shall speak to ye anon.'

'Pigeons,' said James, humiliated. He could bear it no longer, adding lamely: 'Lady, I must go. I must write my sermon…I am…I have been… glad to meet thee.'

'And I, thee.' She turned to go and said: 'Yet I do not know thy name.'

'James Throgmorton, priest of this parish.'

'James,' she repeated. 'I like thy name.' She had thrown a morsel of approval and offering her hand added: 'I am Jessica Fitzgibbon. Perchance shall see thee at thy church on Sunday.'

Before she turned to go, a girl from the draper's shop stumbled from the alleyway, ending their conversation. James bore her up as she sank to the ground. 'Mistress, are ye unwell?'

'Oh, God save me, the shop-keeper turned me out, for I burned so hot.'

Noticing dreadful blotches about her neck and breast, James instantly released the girl from his grip and stood apart. The doctor had lately confided in him about the possibility of the plague reaching London, for a journeyman had talked of the vapours in Amsterdam brought to England in infected goods. Moreover, citizens had gossiped about sickness in St. Giles-in-the-Fields. Only a while since, the bitt-maker was taken with a fever, and now...

'Ye leave her – on the ground?' queried Jessica. 'I am amazed. Come...' She stooped to offer help.

'Nay, lady!' James raised a prohibitive hand: 'She must go apart.' And turning to the sick woman said gently: 'Mistress, ye may take refuge in my church – 'tis but a short walk. I'll go to the physician's house for remedy anon. It seems the doctor finds himself another charge.'

Again, Jessica stepped forward to take the woman's hand, for the poor soul sobbed pitifully. 'I go this way to the back of my house – along Church Lane. She shall take my hand.'

'Nay,' said James. She walks apart. God knows I shall do right,' but the poor girl cried so pitifully that Jessica would have none of it.

'Thus, do I do right. I am a goodly nurse. I did nurse a nestling once – fallen from the tree and a mouse savaged by a cat,' she said, taking the woman's arm. 'She cannot walk well and knows not the time of day.'

The priest thought her uncommonly obstinate but with a certain charm and, when they reached the church, he smiled at her and said: 'Lady – go ye home. The sun is going down. Ye should not walk abroad alone.'

'Then till Sunday,' she said, gently encouraging the poor afflicted woman towards the church in the care of the priest. Then, revealing an impish dimple in her cheek, she smiled and added: 'Now I must go to reprimand my naughty maid.'

James turned and saw that she lived in the big house close by, for he watched her guiding her silk skirt through a gate and noticed that the way was overhung with musk roses all in bud. He stood there, half forgetting who or where he was, until a moan from the sick girl, drooping by his side, reminded him. At once, he turned to the poor soul and, leading her at arms-length through the lynch-gate, told her: 'Lie ye down on the porch bench. I shall to the physician.'

3

James turned into the lane from the church. It was growing dark now and the alleyway was ill-lit, but for a dingy lantern shining from a wall – enough to disclose a group of 'rogues and vagabonds' who crouched beneath the arch. He moved cautiously among them with growing awareness that they were not miscreants at all, but poor servants turned out of doors huddled together for warmth, for the spring evening was growing chill. 'God be with thee,' he said, dropping coins at their feet, and they blessed him as he walked on. Soon he took a shortcut to the physician's house, which he found in the dim lantern light by means of a brass plaque shining on the door: 'George Hartwell, Physician'. He would have rung the bell, but at once hung back, for a wet-nurse, in distress and stinking of sweat – was waiting to be let in. James bided his time.

When the housemaid opened the door, the woman pushed her way to the doctor with great force and purpose. He was pondering over a massive tome debating plague cures when she startled him.

'Doctor!'

He looked up, snatching his spectacles from his face. 'Mistress, ye do intrude!'

'Doctor, doctor, I have a fever and I have given suck.' She clutched at him: 'Give me physic – lest I pass it to the child...'

'A wet-nurse, with a fever – giving suck? Oh, the devil!'

'Give me physic, doctor, give me physic,' she cried,

dropping to the floor. 'For the child's sake, give me physic!'

The doctor called the housemaid and instructed her to take the woman to a small room resembling a surgery. 'Warm some milk, crush two cloves of garlic and mix them in the milk, then bid her rest awhile,' he said.

'What do I then?' asked the housemaid, when all the while the woman with her cried out in pain.

'Do? What shall ye do? Do not pour it on her head. Bid her drink it!'

'What shall ye do then, doctor, for she doth fall about?'

'Examine her and decide, or let blood, and 'twill be yours if I do not get any peace. 'Zounds, I am spent!'

The troubled doctor sat down again amid a scholarly muddle of bottles, jars and dusty books. He leaned over a large tome and resumed his work, weighing up sundry remedies for the plague which may be of help to the woman. They had recently been discussed in a meeting with the Royal College of Physicians; but he couldn't help wondering whether their recommended cures were any better than the quack's – though he consoled himself that at least the physicians' remedies were benign and did not endanger the lives of their patients. They had lately discussed the benefits of conserve of roses, provided they could get hold of any, for the roses were reluctant to bloom in the spring. Yet he considered whether such a concoction would be of any benefit, even if roses could be had. He knew that herbs were of use but questioned their efficacy for the cure of such an extreme infection. Garlic was certainly a potent

13

antiseptic and had its uses...Lavender, perhaps...? He wondered whether it was the herbs that encouraged the insects that carried the plague. He dipped his quill in the ink and began to scratch out his findings. Just then, in accordance with his thoughts, an insect no bigger than a speck of coal dust, hopped onto his notebook and flitted off again so quickly that he could discern neither the nature of the creature nor the irony of it. It was a flea – courtesy of the wet-nurse.

'Insects! They are the cause of this malady!'

His thoughts were interrupted by a heavy knock on the door.

'Dear Lord, give me strength,' said the doctor.

'Doctor, 'tis a clergyman to see ye,' said the housemaid.

'Let him enter.'

As James came through the door, the candles flickered and flared up in the draught, highlighting a human skeleton that seemed to dance from a nearby hook. James winced, for he considered that it had probably danced upon the gallows of late, for the gallows was a rich source of cadavers with which to furnish the medical profession.

'Doctor! I have one sick in my church,' said James urgently.

'God help us!' said the doctor, slamming his book shut.

'I am sorry for this rude intrusion, but...'

'Nay, come in. Come hither, James – and sit ye down.'

'The young girl in my church...'

The doctor looked grave. 'She is in advanced state of

fever?'

'Ay.' She is very sick, doctor.'

The doctor gestured in despair: 'I am only one, James. I cannot cut myself in two. Already a wet-nurse sickens in my care. Anon I must let her blood. I do be sorry, James. I cannot come at once.'

'Then what must I do?'

He reached for a phial on his desk. 'Give her six drops of this physic – 'tis strong. If she doth prevail, come hither in the morn and I shall come to her.'

'I thank thee, doctor.'

'I have worked long and have little stomach left for it now, James.' He reached for a bottle of whisky and showed it to the priest.

'I thank thee, nay,' said James.

'Then I shall see ye on the morrow,' said the doctor. 'For now, I must take pains to see how my patient fares on garlic milk, for still I juggle with my remedies. I shall sleep little tonight.'

'I shall return to try thy remedy and see ye on the morrow.'

James hastened back to the church. When he entered the porch, he was surprised to see the lady Jessica sitting beside the girl and holding a lantern aloft.

'Lady, what do ye here with the sick?'

'I was looking at my roses, when I did see thee leave in the direction of the market square. I came hither to tend her, for knew ye left her all alone.'

'I did but seek out the good doctor for physic. How doth the poor girl?'

'Do ye not see?' she asked, bringing the lantern close

to the girl's face.

It was a ghastly sight. The young woman lay with her fists clenched, eyes and mouth wide and her face blotched with tokens.

James recoiled.

'She hath died in great distress,' said Jessica.

'God have mercy,' said James, crossing himself and uttering a prayer.

Jessica fought back a tear: 'But for the draper, who did cast her out, she had no friends. She did tell me that her name was Ruth. It doth mean compassion.'

He nodded and offered her his hand: 'Come, 'twas a goodly thing ye did, lady. Pray God ye have not caught her malady. Now let me take thee home.'

'It is but across the way. I shall go alone, but first…' She removed her cloak and laid it over the woman's body. 'She hath no winding sheet, and I would that she died with something from a friend.'

'I shall ask my washerwoman to clean it and I shall return it anon,' said James, in the vague hope of seeing her again.

'Nay, I do have another. And I would not trouble ye, for I am certain ye have many wicked souls to save.'

'Lady, there was no need…'

'I bid thee goodnight, priest.'

He watched her go through the lynch-gate and into the lane, the flickering candle-lamp held out before her.

4

Soon after James had left his house the night before, the wet-nurse had expired her last just as the doctor was lancing a large boil. At first, he feared she had died of shock, but consoled himself that she was, by then, far too insensible to have felt it. He would have gone immediately to inspect the infant she had been feeding but had little idea where her family lived. When at last he found the house further down the alley, he heard the tragic sound of weeping and wailing. He returned home, lamenting that he could do nothing to halt the progress of this dreadful disease.

The doctor had risen late and emerged in his study after breakfast wearing a crooked periwig, for he had gone to sleep forgetting that he had it on. He was looking over his thesis: 'Insects Carriers of the Plague' when James arrived.

'Good morrow, doctor.'

'Ah – How now, James?'

'God hath taken the girl. There is no need for ye to come. She hath no relations. Thus, shall I arrange a pauper's burial.'

'Ay, 'tis sad. Yet I must come to establish the true cause of death. It must be entered in the Bill of Mortality.'

'Surely 'twas the plague, doctor? The poor girl looked in fright as though torn from her body betimes. I fear we do have a visitation, for so much sin did return to the city with the restoration of the King, and it hath multiplied since, the gaming houses, the theatres –   exhibiting I know not what. Now 'tis surely the wrath of God.'

'James, James, call it thus, if ye must,' said the doctor. A natural Cavalier, he disdained, though tolerated, the touch of puritanism in his friend.

Yet James was not alone imagining a wrathful God descending from the clouds to visit sickness and death on a sinful city for, barely six years ago, England was still in the grip of the God-fearing Puritans, and they didn't vanish with the return of the King.

'To serious matters,' continued the doctor.

'God's wrath is not serious?'

The doctor rolled his eyes. 'May I be assured of thy confidence, sir?'

'As a man of the cloth,' James promised.

'It must be kept close. We would prevent a hubbub. To the matter.' The doctor took another swig, savoured it, and said quietly: 'Too many burials.'

'Too many? The dead must be buried.'

'Nay, there is a general increase, I'll warrant.'

'Ye do forget, doctor, that funerals are my province. Thereby I have witnessed this, and indeed there shall be more,' he said. 'Daily, the citizens play as they please and truly I fear the hand of God.'

'I know little of the hand of God yet mark ye this: I attended three sick women and two men of late. Other physicians in the city, with whom I did confer and lately did consult, had many more with buboes – swellings beneath the arms and in the groin and other signs of the distemper.'

'I do fear this contagion – 'tis gross.'

'Ay, great swellings, James – blotches and purples and burning fevers. No blood-letting would cure it and no leech feed on it. Mark me, they had the plague.'

James grimaced. 'Uh! Horrible! It is as I feared!' Instinctively, he rose and waved his kerchief across his face. 'There was no doubt?'

'Nay, 'twas no doubt they had the plague. Yet there is mischief in high places, James, for when I studied the bill proclaiming the manner of their deaths, I was agape to see they had recorded the scarlet fever. They did not record the plague. They lie, James.'

'Lord have mercy!'

'Since then, another and another. Spotted fever and a host of other maladies go down upon the list, that I and the good Lord know, for certain, were the plague.'

'Pestilence, 'tis biblical – the retribution of the Lord.'

'I do not know if 'tis retribution. If 'tis true, as I suspect, then there is a great catastrophe ahead of us, James, that they say is written in the stars.'

'There is talk, and 'tis true the augers tell of an ill-reigning star?'

'They do. They say the comet that did tear through the sky in December, trailing vapours, was an ill-omen. I have no time for astrology – the conjunction of the stars, James. Would ye trust stargazers, witches and necromancers? Nay, 'tis hocus-pocus.'

'Ay. I cannot aby the rascals that do scatter it abroad. Yet I have contemplated this. Is it not true that the moon rules the tide, and when it is full it brings with it a madness? Nay, I am without myself – I do not mean the full tide but the moon. But 'tis not for me to ponder. I am a priest who peddles psalms and proverbs. Yet methinks the dog-star is further than the moon, Dear Lord, I am weary and I tie myself in knots!'

'Untie thy knots and listen, James. There have been comets presaging ill before, that have littered the earth with death, disease and disaster. I say, 'tis nothing supernatural but a scientific fact: the comet that did trail the vapour in its wake hath sprayed the earth with insects, and I did see one of the devils in my study only yesternight – on this book,' he said, repeatedly jabbing a finger on the tome.

'Uh, 'tis God's wrathful vengeance!'

'Nay, 'tis science. An eminent physician that I know, experimented thus. He bade the afflicted huff upon a glass and did magnify it. What he did behold, my friend, was horrible – all manner of tiny creatures did squirm upon that glass.'

'Oh, my good Lord!'

'Ay – For myself, I could not aby it.'

'But how can we vanquish these evil creatures?'

'We cannot.'

'Cannot? But surely...'

'They are microscopic, nay, nearly microscopic – and so quick, James, that they do jump away as soon as looking on them and are gone.'

'Horrible, 'tis too horrible. What remedy for this dreadful affliction visited upon us?'

'To lance the swellings and let forth the puss that doth contain the evil.'

'No!'

'Many other preparations are meant to be a cure.'

'The drink, doctor?'

'The physicians have not yet been persuaded, but for myself – there is yet hope for a cure,' he said, indulging in a swig.

'The snuff?'

'Nay, they are not grateful of it. They scoff at all remedies but their own – and 'tis Hawker, James, Hawker that doth set the cat among the pigeons.'

'God be praised for the cat!'

'Desist thy levity, sir – 'tis my domain, not thine.'

'I did forget me – but the pigeons, sir – my wig...'

'Hang thy periwig. These are matters of moment.'

'I repent me. For the physicians – 'tis gross ingratitude to an eminent member of their college.'

'Ay.'

'What new cures do they offer?'

'A conserve of rose – as I have said.'

'It sounds well,' said James, 'yet they shall not be satisfied, for 'tis too early and not a rose hath bloomed. All over London 'tis the same.'

In the distance came the clanging of a bell and the lusty voice of the town crier. 'Ten-of-the-clock and all is well.'

'He shall soon find 'tis not,' said the doctor, in response, 'but keep it to thyself, James – for as long as ye can.'

'Ay, all is not well, and I do feel it in my bones,' and as he uttered it, James looked up at the skeleton that grinned down on him from the corner of the room. He shuddered, for the words 'Memento mori' came to him, and the grin on the skeleton seemed a symbol of death.

5

Most citizens in London Town went about their business unaware that the plague stealthily crept among them, despite the augurs of doom, but as the weeks went by, there were mumbles of suspicion to be heard in the taverns, gaming houses, in the market place… Fewer and fewer ships came to port and mariners, who surely liked to drink after a heavy day unloading their cargoes, now skulked aboard ship.

'Where are the sailors that fill my coffers?' wondered the taverner, counting his coins. 'Few ships are in the port. My ale should flow freely now.'

'Ay, 'tis strange,' said the farrier.

'Strange or no,' grumbled the taverner, 'I do miss the chink o' coin?'

'Ay, and I'll bid ye good morrow, for I have horses to shoe.'

'Will ye not have another?'

'Nay, I'll to work. Business is good at the forge.'

The taverner turned to the tavern wench. 'Bring them in, woman. Do not stand there like a frightened rabbit, for their tankards must be filled. And look ye merry. The tipplers do pay for a smile –The matter, wife?'

'I heard ye, I heard ye! Do not be hard on the wench, for her little lad ails.'

'For that I do be sorry,' said the taverner, 'but the girl must work.'

'Give me the tankards and the ale,' ordered his wife. 'She hath worked her fingers to the bone for a crust. Give the girl a moment with the lad – or have ye a heart o' stone?'

'Ye shall feel my fist,' said her husband, looking up from his coins.

'Nay, ye shall feel mine first,' said his wife, an ample figure of a woman with a good punch. 'Get thee to thy son, Bess.'

Bess shot a scared look towards the taverner.

'Ah, get away with thee,' he said.

In many ways, London Town was thriving. The streets and alleyways remained alive with the chance to make a penny or two and, ignorant of the threat amongst them, still the citizens inhabited the theatres, the taverns, the gaming houses – jostling together – all breathing the same air, all sharing the same cesspools. The gossips were not yet spilling the news of plague...

'Ay, 'tis a strange affair,' said a citizen, 'for we were at the tippling house three days hence. There ne'er was a merrier soul than the bitt-maker – and gone to meet his Maker so soon? They say the cobbler's taken with swellings. I did see him only yesterday to measure my feet for new boots.'

'Yet all is most well with his 'prentice,' said the other.

'Ay, a spirited lad, that doth like to play tricks – 'tis his nephew.'

'Who is the wench he capers with?'

'The seamstress. She makes petticoats for the Lady Castlemaine.'

'Ah, she is a seemly wench.'

'The Lady Castlemaine?'

'Nay, the seamstress. But there's a whore?'

'The seamstress?'

'Nay, the Lady Castlemaine. It would be well for the King to be rid of her.' The citizen took a pinch of snuff and, having done so, inclined his head and directed his mouth towards his friend in a manner of gossip. 'I have heard, from the horse's mouth...'

'And from every other nag in London Town. She plagues him. He has, as his father, lost his head.'

The citizen nodded. 'I have friends at the palace. They say the King plays the sport, then turns to matters of administration with equal countenance. The courtiers flatter him, and 'tis said that never did a man play tennis in such a dull fashion yet, when he hits an ill shot, they clap and cry out with one voice: "Well done, sir! Well done!" They are fools.'

'Ay, 'tis a wonder he's not sick of it. Yet I profess I would not wish ill of the monarch.'

'Nay, for 'tis the only way. We have seen the ill that regicide brings – 'tis a sin and 'twill be paid for come the Judgement.'

'Ay. And something else I have observed. Last week... What the devil?'

'Jack Hogg – He that occupies the stocks more often than his hovel. We'll to the coffee house.'

'Ay, I did forget my nosegay and the air begins to stink.'

'The wretch stinks more than Fleet Ditch that doth overflow with feculence.'

'Or a cesspool that doth swarm with flies in a heatwave. I dare swear 'twas he that cut my purse in the market place.'

'Ay, yet 'tis wonder he hath not been caught.'

'My uncle is a magistrate. He says Jack Hogg doth slip the noose but not the stocks, for they cannot catch him in his ungodly acts – unless he doth breach the peace.'

'Which he hath done marvellously well, for again they do drag him to the stocks.'

6

There were miscreants in London, then, but never did a soul keep the constables busier than Jack Hogg. He was never caught for the evil he did – be it as cutpurse, horse thief or murderer. He was a cunning wretch who knew well how to avoid the gibbet for a heinous crime, but never the stocks for disturbing the peace. He was a familiar face in the square and, such was his popularity, that no upright citizen would call Jack Hogg a pig for fear of insulting the creature, and his infamy continued to go before him. Now, once again, he came tied with a rope, rough-handled by the law.

'Ow! Ah! Bastard! Bum crack!' he cried, kicking and wriggling like a trapped animal. 'Let me free, you filthy…'

Two constables wrestled with the wretched man until he was locked tight in the stocks, leaving him with tears of self-pity mingling with the grime on his face.

'Shut thy ugly mouth or I'll lock ye up for good,' warned the constable in charge and, turning into an alley, told his companion: 'I'll no more of him. My wife runs a fever and I must to the apothecary for remedy. They tell me, rue – or garlic in the mouth.'

'Nay, 'tis wormwood.'

Trapped in the stocks, Jack Hogg sniffed and looked about him. His eyes darted about until they alighted on the good doctor and the clergyman. He strained his ears so he might hear their conversation.

'Jack Hogg!' complained the doctor. 'Was there ever a more unworthy knave? Best clap him in irons and leave him there, or nail his ears up to the pillory. And this from a gentle soul such as I.'

Across the way, Jack Hogg, feigning sleep, opened his cunning eye.

'My sentiments, sir. Jack Hogg's a horse thief and a cut-purse – though the devil himself prove it. On his best behaviour, he idles his time in taverns and gaming houses,' complained James, 'Naught can you tell me about the wretch I do not already know.'

They sat for a while exchanging news and opinions by the watering pump, shadows lengthening with the sinking sun.

'I tell thee, 'twas in the tavern – where I had gone to give physic...'

'Did ye give the physic or get it, doctor?' James smiled wryly.

'I had not a dram,' objected the doctor. 'Ye do interrupt. Ay. The drunken sot did fall upon the table corner and split his head, whereupon Bess, his woman, screamed and hollered as 'twere Doomsday – such was a little blood augmented by her imagination. Upon which, confusion upon confusion, and all attracted to himself by himself in that confusion.'

'Indeed 'twas a confused time, doctor!' Nonchalantly, James changed the subject. 'Dost know the lady, Jessica?'

'Ay, the daughter of the silk merchant with the kibes...'

'The kibes?' James was at once startled. 'The daughter hath kibes on her toes?'

'Nay, nay – 'tis her father hath the kibes. They swell up scarlet and do drive him mad with itching.'

James sighed with relief, for the lady's feet were sacred. 'The lady Jessica,' he continued, 'is a lovely – though recalcitrant lady.'

'To the point, priest. Tell me what the lady Jessica hath to do with wretch of wretches, Jack Hogg?'

'Jack Hogg accosted her when she did arrive in town.'

'The more the wretch! But do not blame the lady, James.'

'Nay, I do not blame the lady, for surely she is virtuous.'

'Then how is she recalcitrant?'

'She plagues me,' said James – troubled. 'She hath no respect for a man of the cloth.'

'Respect must be earned – even by a man of the cloth,' noted the doctor.

'I object to that, sir, for I have done nothing to earn her disrespect.'

'Not so hot! Ye are touch-paper to a cannon, sir.'

'Then I beg thy pardon, sir.'

The doctor stood up. 'Enough tittle-tattle. I must to the apothecary for plasters...'

'And I to the church. I have a sermon to prepare – though on what theme I know not. Perchance the sins of the fathers? Nay, something in it lacks,' and, catching Jack Hogg looking his way, he called out: 'Repent, ye Jack Hogg, or take upon ye the vengeance of the Lord!'

'I am God-feared,' jeered Jack as they passed. He squirmed as he said it, for a group of ragamuffin children, in teasing mood, appeared and accosted him.

'Ha! Ha! Look, 'tis Jack Hogg!'

'What d' ye do, Jack?'

A big girl with tangled hair, weighed in and kicked the stocks.

'Get off!' shrieked Jack, whereupon a tiny boy, emboldened by his companions, stamped up from the edge of the group. 'I'm going to twist thy nose.' But he had awoken the devil.

'Twist my nose and wait till I'm loose, an hour hence and I'll string ye up to the nearest gibbet and pull thy innards out. I'll come at night and string thee up. Do ye hear?' he thundered.

'No Jack!' quaked the tiny child and scampered away.

But the big girl thrust her hands on her hips and dared him: 'Ye can't scare us Jack Hogg. Let him have it!' And tipping a deal of rubbish over him, all three scampered off in triumph.

'Bah! I'll have thee for supper, thou little pip-squeaks!' he thundered, just as a constable appeared with a bucket of water from the butt, sloshed the rubbish off and left him spitting curses.

'Ow!' Jack raved, at once squinting to see his wary wife, Bess the tavern wench, approach.

Bess needed to approach Jack warily, for he had abused her for years; humiliating her, taunting her, striking her – blaming her for everything that went wrong with his abominable life. For six years she had endured it, ever since he kicked her in the belly when she was carrying their child. A monster would have treated her with greater kindness, but she would not leave him. She told herself that he couldn't help it. It was always somebody else's fault, or the drink made him act the way he did, or his ill-behaviour was due to some other incomprehensible reason, but what Bess really felt was the universal need to be loved. Orphaned when she was a young girl, she had met Jack at a horse fair on a common outside the city walls. She had gone to public gatherings often, hoping to find some gentleman's boots to clean. She had earned almost a shilling and was turning it over in her grubby hands when a symbolic shadow fell on the ground before her, and Jack Hogg tapped her on the shoulder. He was a strapping lad then, crudely handsome, and the scruffy girl, who answered to the name of Bess, looked up at him with big, trusting eyes. 'Thou 'rt a pretty lass,' he told her. She smiled, for she had never been called pretty before. 'Let me borrow ye, but ye must keep mum,' he winked. He looked about him for an opportunity – for he lived by his wits – and sweeping the girl up to sit her on a piebald horse, said: 'My sister wants to try the mare,' and wearing a charming smile, he told the horse to walk on. Once on the edge of a gathering crowd, he jumped on the back of it with the girl and galloped apace into London Town. Such was the beginning of her fearful life with the rogue, Jack Hogg. When she skivvied in the tavern, he called her idle, and though she was ever faithful to him, he beat her for making eyes at anyone whose tankard of ale she had filled...

'Poor Jack!'

'Ay, poor Jack – 'tis always Jack Hogg. Nobody likes his face! Nobody likes his face!'

'I do,' promised the poor tavern wench. 'I like your face, Jack.'

He looked to an advantage, dripping with self-pity.

'What d' ye want, wench? What does anybody want with me?'

'To give thee comfort, Jack,' she said gently, lifting the corner of her apron and dabbing his face.

'Comfort! Comfort! Ye brought me to a pretty cesspool, and 'twere not for those fluttering eyelashes…'

'No Jack,' she winced. 'I never did, I do swear – by the Book.'   '

By the Book?' he jibed. Bess could neither read nor write, but she had heard the priest read from it and took some comfort in a prayer. 'The devil would be more comfort. Now scratch my neck. I've been eaten alive by fleas. Scratch till it hurts. Higher – not so high. Clapped in the stocks and can't scratch my neck – and now I want to piss! … My father taught me how to cozen, I dare swear. I've had it hard and there's the truth,' he whined.

'I do know, Jack,' Bess sympathised. 'He gave thee naught but grief.'

'All I wanted from life was a bit o' fun. What's the use of life without a game or two – without a tankard of ale and a pair of warm thighs?'

'Oh, Jack, do not talk thus!'

'Life asks too much of me and there's the shame of it.'

'Oh, poor Jack,' said Bess stroking his wiry hair. 'Ay, 'twill be a happy day when somebody understands Jack Hogg.' She put a cup of milk to his lips. 'Here, drink this.'

'What is 't?'

'Milk to build thy strength – mine own, Jack.'

'Milk? Bah!' He spat it back. He spat all her kindness back.

The poor girl had a child and scarcely money to buy food to give to the delicate soul, except for a penny or two from the tavern. Long she had endured the abuse for the child's sake, unwisely believing that the kinder she was to the oaf, the more she would endear herself to him. But her kindness by some strange, ill-psychology, only irritated Jack Hogg more.

'Come here,' he rasped. 'Did I blacken thine eye?'

'Ay, Jack,' she winced.

'Ye did deserve it.'

'Nay! Please, please do not say that, for 'tis shame – and it did vex the lad.'

'Where is the lad?' asked Jack.

'Poor little Jim be sick today. I left him with the inn-keeper. I must go to him now for he doth need me.'

'Need ye, Jim? What? He's never been more than a bundle o' trouble.'

Bess suddenly rose in strength to defend the boy. 'Nay, he be a good lad, a gentle soul...'

'Gentle? Nah, 'twill be knocked out of him!'

'Ye do not – ye cannot mean these things, Jack, for 'tis the drink maddening thy blood.'

'What else have I?' he snarled.

She clutched at anything to mollify him: 'Who knows, but the inn-keeper will make thee ostler when Will goes.'

The moment she said it, the inn-keeper's wife came hurrying into the square: 'Get thee to thy boy,' she said urgently. 'He sickens worse and calls for thee.'

'No! Oh, Jack, I must to little Jim now.'

Jack shook his head and seeing her go, closed his eyes and nodded in the clasp of the stocks. He roused when the town crier rang seven-of-the-clock and proclaimed all well. Soon afterwards there came the rattle of keys, and the constable, loudly remonstrating, set him free.

7

Jack, snatching at the talk of plague, took to the streets to whisper it abroad. There were always gullible strangers in London Town: visiting dignitaries, journeymen, adventurers …. Pulling them aside, he would tell of ancient remedies that could cure beggars and kings alike, and how he could conjure them up. In this manner, in colourful distraction, he carefully cut purses and with a hullaballoo cried out 'Thief!' pointing and giving chase to deflect the guilt. It was an old trick of many an old rogue but his activity was not always fruitful, for some – such as the journeyman in silk – were wise to the tricksters and had other money secreted in the hidden pockets of their jackets. Such was the event that drew the journeyman into conversation with James…

'Good morrow, priest.'

'Good morrow, sir. Ye seem distracted.'

'My purse hath been cut. Though 'tis surely the thief's ill-fortune. It had but a farthing in it.'

'God be praised – 'tis fortunate for thee,' said James, raising a hand in blessing.

'Tell me, 'tis true ye have the plague in Town?' asked the journeyman.

'How do ye ask?'

'The cut-purse did say.'

'He it is that plagues us, for we know not who he is. He is like a shadow and hath not yet been caught. But to the question. There are but a few with fever.'

'Then I shall buy rue.'

'Nay, repentance – 'tis only this preserves thee from the plague. Ye are lately in London Town?'

'Ay. I journey in silk for the merchant, Fitzgibbon. I am here betimes,' he said and, with a rakish grin laced with innuendo, he delivered his intention: 'I fain would woo his lovely daughter.'

A sudden enmity shot through the priest. He fixed his smile and quickly reminded himself that jealousy was akin to envy, and thus a sin. Yet why did his cheeks flush with uninhibited fury at the thought of another man wooing the lady Jessica? He hardly knew her. This was the devil's work! He composed himself, but there was an edge to his voice as he said 'It pleases Providence to give ye a chance to repent if ye so need.'

'Repent, sir? How so?'

'To protect ye – from anything ye do need to be protected from,' he said, puzzled at his own answer.

'I do not need to be protected from the lady, sir,' said the journeyman.

'Perchance the lady doth need to be protected from ye!' said James, alarming himself.

'Nay, ye are too thorough at thy work. I shall adjourn to the Fitzgibbon house. I bid thee good day, priest.'

'God go with thee,' said James, nodding with decorum. But he smarted, and such were the thoughts that maddened his blood that he wished he had never taken holy orders. He watched him walk away, and what he beheld next threw him into a greater agony of jealousy, for he saw the silk merchant who, only moments ago had been intent on wooing her, hail the lady Jessica as she turned from the lane into the square.

'Without this collar,' James told himself, 'I might have punched that man in the face!' Surely, he thought, the devil had borrowed his tongue. But he was brought back to penitence when a poor old woman came his way weeping.

'What ails ye, woman?'

'Oh, sir,' wailed the poor soul, 'my brother and his wife and child were taken sudden sick a week hence and did die this morn.'

'God help us!' said James, making the sign of the cross. 'What was the nature of their malady?'

'They say the spotted fever, sir.'

James had divided his attention and, with an anxious eye on the progress of the journeyman, was glad to see that he had gone on his way.

'It grieves me so I know not what to think or say,' continued the woman, 'Their child was only six. Their little child was only six.'

'For that I am truly sorry,' said James who, looking aslant, saw Jessica standing nearby. Words floated about him and he struggled to console the woman. 'Yet – do not grieve, woman, for 'tis God's will – they do but sleep – they shall sleep until the dreadful Day of Judgement.' He pointed the way and said hurriedly: 'Go yonder to my church, where I shall comfort thee anon.'

'Ay, sir, I shall seek comfort in God's house,' said the poor soul and, bowing her head in grief, she shuffled away.

'Good morrow, priest,' said Jessica.

'Good morrow, lady,' he said, feeling his cheeks burn, 'Ye are, I trust, well.'

'A little hot, 'tis the sun.' She opened out the fan that dangled from her wrist and waved it across her face.

'Ay, 'tis the sun,' he said, grateful for an excuse to hide his blush.

'Forgive me, I did not intend – It seems I could not avoid overhearing thy counsel,' she said. 'The woman was in great distress and yet ye preached to her.'

'Ye do confuse me, lady. I am a preacher. Therefore, I do preach.'

Then with all her courage she challenged him: 'Ye preach without care.'

'Nay.'

'Ay. Pray tell me why a little child of six, yet innocent about the ways of men, should yet be judged?'

'It is not my duty to question the word of the Lord.'

'Is it not thy duty to question the truth?'

'Lady, ye are audacious!'

'The poor woman was in grief and ye did not comfort her.'

Suddenly, he faltered in her presence. She had turned his perception of himself upside down. He searched for words, then looked up to the sky in fear: 'I ask thee not to speak thus...'

'I see no thunder in the clouds. The sky is blue and the birds do sing. Have ye not heard how beautifully they sing? It seems I have another God than thine. The journeyman...'

'What of the journeyman?'

'He did say ye were a fire and brimstone priest...'

'The varlet!'

'But I did berate him for his gossip. I do not scoff at

friends,' she said, closing her fan. She had disarmed him in a moment. 'Sir, Good day,' and with a rustle of silk had gone into the market place.

James sank down on a bench, all energy gone. While stroking his brow, he noticed the good doctor hurrying to the apothecary. 'Doctor, good morrow.'

'Good morrow,' and seeing his friend slumped and alone, asked: 'What ails ye, James – are ye unwell?'

'Nothing a little blood-letting or hungry leech cannot cure.'

'How so?'

'My blood is hot – a strange distemper.'

'Pray God 'tis not the plague!'

'She it is that plagues me – the lady, Jessica.'

'I have met the family. They are respected.' The doctor took a healthy swig from his flask. 'The lovely Jessica doth mean well.'

'Mean well? If the lady Jessica means well, then I am the devil!'

'Ha! But I have little time for this. Jack Hogg hath stirred the news abroad, and 'tis as I thought – the plague, James, 'tis the plague, though every day they hide the nature of the malady.'

'Dear Lord!'

'Hogg is a chaos-monger. Mark me, there'll be a general hubbub – lest the Lord Mayor intervene. Take heart, my friend. I must hasten to the apothecary and ye to church.'

8

There were few cases of plague in the spring, but a sense of foreboding still crept among a few superstitious citizens who looked for signs, listened to augurs, heeded God. Some began to gather herbs, hang garlic about the house, make sweet smelling pomanders and posies and store up victuals, for many had heard tales of the black death and other plagues that had swept through Europe in past times, and were busy making themselves ready. But for most, who were fortunate to have a living, London Town remained a playground, particularly for the youth then, whose high spirits were adjudged loose morals in some priestly quarters, destined to elicit the wrath of their Maker. Such a reputation attached itself to Samuel, the shoemaker's apprentice, and the little seamstress, Mopsa...

'Come Mopsa, sew my shirt,' said Samuel, grabbing her by the arm.

'I'll none of it.'

'Ye did tear it.'

'Ye provoked me,' she said, shaking him off.

'Mistress,' he objected, 'Ye provoke me day and night.'

'I'll none of thy night, sir!' she teased. 'Ye sit and sew shoes all day, so ye can sew thy shirt.'

She punched him and he grabbed her arms.

'I do but wax the thread, run errands and soften the leather for thy pretty little feet.'

'I can kick with my pretty little feet,' she said – and did so.

'Ow! Mopsa, I do but learn the trade. I sew seldom and very little.'

'Ye do so very little,' she countered, careless of her own wit.

Samuel looked to the ground and feigned hardship: 'Mopsa, ye wrong me, indeed ye do. Thy delicate little stitches do become a lady.'

She laughed and gave chase. He caught her and they kissed – just as James came round the corner.

'What d' ye do?'

'That which desires to be done, sir,' said Samuel.

'Unhand the maiden, unhand her, I say!'

'I shall not be unhanded,' objected Mopsa.

'Fore God, he kisses ye!'

'Ye do interfere, sir!'

'Ay, that he does. We'll to the tavern, for my master is sick and knows not where I am,' laughed Samuel. Then with hands intertwined, they cut through the alley.

James stood perplexed for a while, wondering whether the world had grown mad, for, on a sudden, it appeared that those in it showed scant respect for a minister of the church. Were he a fortune teller, he thought, he would be sworn that he was ruled by the whim of a star. He looked up, and surely the brightness of a star looked down on him.

'Ye do interfere, sir, indeed ye do.'

'Mischief upon another mischief!'

'I do come to make amends,' said Jessica, 'for 'tis not your fault...'

'What mean ye?' Then, calming himself, he took her in his confidence. 'Lady, let us not quarrel. There is no time to behave thus. I would confide in thee – something of moment. Know that 'tis as we suspected. There is a plague toward.'

'I did already think it so.'

James nodded and drew closer. 'Ay, but 'tis an evil visitation. Do not spill the news abroad. It is best ye leave Town with thy family or take provisions, shut thyself within doors and be penitent.'

'God knows I have done no ill, sir.'

'May it please Him ye have not. Now do as I say and go thither.'

'I go where I please,' she argued as she walked away.

'Mark me!' he called to her and noticed Jack Hogg skulking by the water pump.

'Now there's a spirited little wench!' jibed Jack.

'She is a lady, Jack Hogg.'

'A rounded little wench, I'll warrant.'

'She is no wench. I'll none of this, thou miserable sinner. If, I say, if, there is a plague toward, as ye do spit abroad, ye must get down on thy knees and beg forgiveness.'

'My sins, my sins, 'twill take me a year to purge them all,' he laughed, 'then I'll turn around and seek another year's worth! I'm past all care. Yet at least I know who I am and there's not many o' them can say that. Dost know thyself? Well, if ye don't, I do. The Devil the Puritan, that's what ye are.'

'Enough, Jack Hogg.'

'And to the point, Sir Parson. Dost know what she is? She is a whore,' he provoked.

'Enough of this!'

41

'Get her on her knees…'

'Desist, I say!'

'And make here repent.'

Purple with rage, James collected himself for form's sake. 'Jack Hogg, thou knave, I know a bunch of sins to hang ye as the rat ye are tomorrow.'

'Ay, that I know,' said Jack, 'but I thank ye not, for 'tis sure thy God will hound me when the time is right.'

'Till then, 't would be kinder to remember thy little one – an innocent in the world. Now repent ye for your sins before 'tis too late.'

'I am God-feared! I am God-feared!' squealed Jack in mock prayer and, spitting venom, made for the alehouse.

'And I am God-feared,' whispered James to himself, 'for the pestilence moves apace, and I do fear for us all.'

9

In 1665, heaping suffering upon suffering, came a blight other than the plague, a swarm of swindlers and cheats that, without compunction, robbed the sick and the poor for their pennies by means of worthless pills and potions. Moreover, there were many victims who did not die of pestilence, but of the poisonous concoctions they had purchased in good faith. The herb sellers were innocent enough, but quacks and mountebanks saw an opportunity to exploit the terrified Londoners, angering the growing number of physicians who sought to bring medicine into good repute. Sadly, even some of the physicians' remedies left much to be desired, but most meant well enough. Some agreed that insects were the cause – and fleas there were aplenty. While, fortunately for the good doctor, there were some who owned that a hearty swig of alcohol doubled as prevention and cure. He was about to knock some back when a quack came through the arch of the alley and took up a pitch on a platform in the square – disseminating his lies...

'Come buy my cordial, 'tis newly sent from Holland,' promised the quack.

The doctor strode up and challenged him. 'Then if 'tis newly sent from Holland, sir, 'tis newly infected with plague. Ye have no licence to practise. Be off with ye.'

'Who are ye to challenge me thus?' objected the quack.

'A doctor and a scholar, sir, of the Royal College of Physicians – formerly of the university of Oxford. I shall inform ye that on this day, we have been charged by the Privy Council of King Charles II, to procure authentic remedies. Ye are not one of our eminent society, sir, and if I take a bottle of that potion to the apothecary to examine, ye shall be damned with it – for, I warrant, it is naught but coloured water. Be off with ye, lest I shall call the constable to clap thee in the pillory.'

'Ye have no remedies, doctor,' barked the quack, disappearing down the back alley.

'No remedies?' objected the doctor to himself, at last secreting the flask of whisky from his inner pocket, a remedy little endorsed by his eminent peers. Yet again, he had no time to savour it, for a citizen called to him urgently.

'Doctor, hasten hither!'

'The matter?'

'The sailmaker's wife doth run a fever and she cried out pitifully with the pain.'

'Show me the way.'

'Thither through Duck alley.'

'Anon I come.' Then noticing Jessica and her maid leaving the hatter's shop close by, he said at once: 'Good morrow Lady, I trust I find thee well. Forgive me, but I cannot stop to pass the time of day.'

'That I do understand, good doctor, for ye needs must tend the sick...'

And the doctor hastened on his way.

'He is a goodly soul and merry, Peg,' she told her maid.

'Ay, that I do know,' said Peg, 'for he doth tend the master's kibes.'

'My father's kibes! They do be horrible, for they put him in ill-humour. Ah, 'tis the herb seller.'

The herb seller came from the shadows, a bunch of fresh rue in her hand: 'Wilt buy my herbs of grace and rue, lady?'

'I have seen ye selling flowers, mistress,' said Jessica. Have ye no roses to perfume the air, for mine do not yet bloom?'

'I do be sorry, lady, there be no roses, for 'tis true they are not yet in bloom,' and offering her a bunch of herbs arranged in a posy said: 'They say there is a plague toward. It is but rosemary and rue will save thee.'

'I do have herbs in my own garden, but thine are a pretty posy,' said Jessica and, pressing a coin in the herb seller's hand, she took the posy before departing with her maid. The herb seller counted the coins but, noticing the priest making his way to the church, she shrank back again and covered her basket.

'Ye have nothing to fear from me,' said James, 'for I know ye from church and ye are a virtuous soul. I see no evil in thy fresh herbs. They do but flavour food and perfume the air, and the doctor says that they do fortify against the plague. Ye shall sell thy herbs with honesty.' He turned away, to see Jessica returning with her maid.

'I do be sorry,' said Jessica to the herb seller. 'I did forget me – for I must buy another for my maid.' She took a posy and turning to James said: 'It seems we are in each other's way, and 'tis strange that once again I overhear thy conference. Yet ye did speak well then.'

'It pleases me to have thy respect. Yet I see ye do not heed my warning, for still ye walk abroad. I beg thee, lady, to mark what I have said.'

'I do thank thee for thy care, sir. Come Peg, we shall go home.'

As she walked away, her little maid trotting beside her dangling a hat-box, she looked back at James. She knew that he had turned to watch her go and, with a smile that put the wonted dimple in her cheek, she disappeared around the corner into the lane. He would have followed her, but for the two poor labourers who approached him in distress.

'What can we do, sir?'

'What ails ye?'

'We have no plague, sir.'

'Then 'tis best ye stay indoors with thy provisions till the visitation is past.'

They were at once downcast. 'We have been cast out and have no place to go, sir.'

James considered them carefully, then said: 'The sexton doth need grave diggers. If ye can use a shovel, go ye to the graveyard and tell him I did send ye. The church will give thee alms.'

'Ay, we thank thee, sir.'

'Ye may thank God,' said James, 'Go to. Ah, doctor!'

The good doctor, coming from the gate of a house along the lane, mopped his brow and shook his head: 'It hath not been merry May, for 'tis growing worse, James.'

'God is angry,' said James, 'and I shudder to think what His dreadful hand may do.'

'Your God is mighty strange, priest,' said the doctor, taking a swig.

'Mighty, but not strange, sir.'

'Ay, strange. Methought he was a God of love whose son doth forgive our sins,' observed the doctor.

'Did he not also say, "Get thee behind me Satan"? Is that not true of the wretched sinner Jack Hogg and the devil's brew he sups with?'

'But the worthy citizens of London Town are not Jack Hogg or his devil's brew, James, thus I cannot believe the wrath of God comes down upon them. Do ye not see that thy God is unjust, James?'

'Ye do leave me disarmed, doctor.'

'Ah – 'tis well. Think on it. But I am a physician, not a theologian, my friend, and should not argue thus,' said the doctor. 'Ah! Still no periwig, priest?'

'I durst not purchase one for fear – lest they should shave the heads of the dead and sell it to the wig makers.'

'Ay, 'tis wise, very wise, for I do know 'tis true. But the wig makers shall not be free from the plague if there are insects in that hair.'

'Horrible, Doctor.'

'Remedies, James, remedies. Do ye take snuff? Once in the nostrils – 'tis my new theory that it filters the miasma.'

'Miasma, Doctor?'

'The infected air, sir.'

'Ah. 'I thank thee, but I do not sniff in that – stuff.'

'Perhaps ye chew it in the mouth?'

'Nay, I do not chew it.'

'Now that the news spreads abroad,' asked the doctor at length, 'what intend ye to do? Wilt thou stay or seek some safer haven?'

'Would that I could, for I am faint of heart and know not what to do. The vicar hath already left, for he did ail with dropsy and fear the plague would see him out.'

The doctor looked suddenly grave. 'Then the good Lord hath need of thee, James. Daily the priests pack up and leave the city, for their burden is too great. So too do the physicians. Sir Philip Hawker led the charge. I shall stay yet with the sick, for what I am worth, and choke the devil plague with this,' he said, uncorking the flask and taking another swig. 'But be sure, we cannot idle. I shall see thee anon, for there goes thy cross to bear.'

'Anon, Doctor. What mean ye – my cross to bear?' The doctor, hurrying on his way, had noticed Jessica turn into the lane towards the church.

10

Jessica was kneeling deep in prayer by the altar when James arrived through the vestry door. He took up some prayer books and began placing them among the pews. After he had placed them, he returned to the altar and came upon her suddenly as she prayed. When she opened her eyes and looked up at him, her curls covered in lace, he took her for a vision and could not speak at once…

'Jessica – what mean ye here?

'What mean I? I was praying to God.'

'Ah – 'tis good that ye repent.'

'Why need I repent?'

'Then why do ye pray?'

'I pray to my God – for the poor and the sick – not for myself, for I am past redemption. Am I not? There is no greater sinner in the whole of London Town than I, if ye are to be believed.'

'Lady…' He sat down beside her, and softening said: 'Ye should not stir abroad.'

'I shall stir abroad if I please.'

'Whither do ye go?'

'To the victuallers,' she said.

'To the victuallers?' And looking down he saw that she had two large empty baskets on the floor by her side. 'But where are thy servants?'

'Our housekeeper hath left town, the cook, the scullery maid and the gardener have taken sick of a sudden and are sent to the pest-house. All are gone – except for little Peg. Poor Peg. I do not think she is sick, but she hath too much burden.'

'Heaven!' He removed his kerchief as though to cover his face. 'What will ye do now?' he asked.

'Escape your God's wrath.'

'Nay, God is not angry with thee,' he said, remembering the conversation with his friend.

'What is this that ye do blow hot and cold?'

'I do grow warm,' he said, with meaning. 'Will ye leave London Town?'

'Ay. My family prepares to leave.'

'Whither?'

'From one penitence to the next. I have an uncle – a pious country parson close by Huntingdon. He offers us the coach house. My other uncle is a lord with an estate in the north – too far away.' Her matter-of-fact tone changed suddenly to one of tender emotion, 'Oh, would that I could stay...'

'Ye would stay?' He eagerly cut in because he hoped she longed to stay for his sake and was about to impress her with a painful sacrifice: 'I would not have thee stay for my sake!' But suspended in the joy of her reply, he fell to earth: '... to nurse the sick,' she concluded.

'To nurse the sick?'

'Ay, I do have a talent for healing. I did cure a sparrow with witch hazel – for it had bruised its wing. Oh, what a joy to see it fly away!'

His hopes had flown away.

Recovering from his disappointment and feeling for a moment bold, he took her hand in his and said. 'Ye are a goodly soul, Jessica...'

'Ye are contrary!' She released her hand.

'And so are ye. Yet I am glad. Truly I am glad ye do decide to go.' Even now he caught himself in the sin of lying and modified his words. 'Ay, 'tis wise, lady.' He paused, then asked: 'Tell me, why do ye scoff at God?'

'I scoff at thy God.'

'He is all one.'

'Nay, with two faces like a Janus – one side good, the other evil? The evil rears its head.'

'Why think ye thus?'

'I shall tell thee. Once I did see – and I shall never forget it – a stone of sorrow upon a bleak and lonely hillside. Beneath that stone – a mark of disrespect – there lay the innocent bones of children, unbaptised, for they were born betimes and died ere they had cried. Imagine how their mothers wept and pleaded with the priests, yet in God's name were scorned and ridiculed.'

'I know of the place – 'tis but an ancient monument in Pict stone.'

'And now? Now where is the Church's sympathy?'

'The Church doth many good works…'

'And many ill. And more – The Church speaks ill of nuns that do roll up their sleeves and help the sick – in protest that they do enhance their souls!'

'I do not – 'tis not…'

'Yet more…'

'Lady!'

'When the plague first struck – and this you know is true – I did hear of a poor man who was so sad and distracted by the death of his wife, so beside himself with grief, that he did hang himself upon a butcher's hook. Thy church, in its infinite mercy, hauled him through the door feet first! He now lies buried where the four roads meet – unhallowed ground at Waltham Cross. His mother sighed and cried and howled, clawing at his unmarked grave of shame. What kind of God is thine, sir? Ye ask me why I scoff at God – 'tis this that grieves me.'

'Ye leave me without a prayer?'

'Nay, I leave thee to think of it, sir.'

For a moment they looked at each other, transfixed, until a cry came from beyond the lane: 'Oh, death! death! death!'

11

In the heat of the summer, the black smoke that issued from flaming coal fires and cressets, curled and hung choking the air along with the noxious fumes of brimstone – its liquid flame emitting an eerie light at night-time. These hellish little infernos were designed to purge the city of the dreadful visitation that bore down on it from a wrathful God.

There was little movement in the Town now. No children played, no dogs frisked and barked. Many of the little ones had died, and dogs and cats that would have routed the black rats that caused the plague, along with other creatures deemed carriers of pestilence – had been snatched and killed without mercy. Yet the close streets and alleyways were not silent; a whimper, a cry for deliverance, a scream, a call for the dead, the clanging of a bell, the trundle of dead-cart wheels... All in all, came the dismal sounds of despair. Did they truly believe it possible that a creator of beauty and harmony had created chaos and dystopia in its stead? This surely was the devil's work.

There were those who argued and questioned their idea of God, but most quaked in fear of Him. Since his acquaintance with Jessica, James began to doubt what he preached, for his words rang hollow, while his good friend prayed – not to a wrathful – but to a kindly God...

'A child snatched ere she hath seen three miserable years of life and taken betimes to the grave. Another, sucking at his mother's breast did suck the milk of death,' said the doctor sombrely, 'and they go together to their grave.'

'Ay, 'tis Heaven's lucky day when a child is taken, but what of Heaven that doth send us Hell? I do confess, I no longer understand the things I preach but waver searching for a God I cannot find,' said James.

'Ay, yet 'tis not God's work, but from the devil that doth creep up from beneath the earth to the clouds to spray the air with insects – yet many do blame God.'

James looked upwards, as though expecting a bolt of lightning to strike him down. 'Nay, nay, we cannot blame the good Lord, sir. The sin is ours.'

'Nay. Do not preach to me, James. I shall not aby it.'

'I do not preach, I cannot preach. We are all of us confused.' His mind, in turmoil, vacillated from one notion to another. He trod carefully, for tempers were raw. 'I have seen ye merrier, doctor,' he said at last.

'Ay, I have so been, but 'tis the infant mortality sears my heart,' he said mournfully. 'I can no longer bear it – though the nature of my profession behoves me to,' he said, offering his companion a drink. 'I do tell thee, 'tis as good protection as any – pickling whatever 'tis that creeps into our blood to cause this malady.'

James raised a prohibitive hand: 'Nay, 'tis all yours, sir.'

'All mine? None, 'tis empty!' discovered the doctor in alarm.

'My prayers are empty,' sighed James. 'I have never known such sadness, and I confess I know not what to say to my flock – yet send them to my church to pray where I cannot.'

'I do confess that I have prayed of late James, for

compassion. How strange that I, a Cavalier at heart who seldom thought on' t, should turn my thoughts so piously to God. Yet it seems, of a sudden, ye begin to doubt. But to the purpose,' he said, inspecting the latest Bill of Mortality nailed to the board. 'The devil!'

'What matter?'

'A greater grief,' lamented the doctor. 'The bill proclaims a deadly increase.'

'God's mercy!' cried James, fearfully. We are too burdened with the dead and dying. Already the graveyard is filling up. What can we do for help? So many have left the city to go to the country or...'

'Ay,' said the doctor. 'The Lord Mayor did tell me that the King, the Court and all his retinue have left London to preserve themselves and do sojourn in Salisbury — thence to Oxford.'

'That I do know,' said James, 'I did witness the procession leave through the gates. So too do Lords and Ladies and a host of gentlefolk leave. The King doth start an avalanche and more are bound to follow. Soon few will be left to help but rogues and vagabonds! What shall we do?'

'Bide our time and do what we must. I do trust the Lord Mayor, for he is wise and doth have a goodly administration. They do appoint examiners of health and searchers to seek out the dead. They say that there will be no going forth from London without a bill of health,' said the doctor.

'Why so?'

'Surely 'tis plain. For the plague increases and the situation grows graver by the day. They do fear the contagion spreading its foul vapours across the whole of England.'

James paused uneasily. 'What would ye say, Doctor, if I told thee that I have contemplated – nay, decided – to leave? There is little I can do now, for my church is nearly empty,' he added, justifying himself. 'Would ye sign my bill of health?'

'Thy church is still a sanctuary for desperate souls, yet ye care not for the few? Oh, 'tis a matter for your conscience, sir, for there hath been a shameful exodus of physicians and clergymen this very day. Would ye run away with a motley crowd of lily-livered cowards, James?' In a tone of disappointment, he added 'For thy bill of health, 'tis not for me to sign, 'tis the mayor's lot,' and licking his lips spontaneously added 'I have spent some merry hours with Sir John over a goodly wine. I doubt not that he would give thee leave.' He flicked a lacy cuff 'Go if ye must.'

The doctor's tone had shaken James. His face flamed red, for never had he felt such shame and, noticing the effect on his friend, the doctor said 'There is no cause for fire and brimstone, James. Ye need only hit the mark, and I would bid thee stay.'

'In that ye do well, sir. I may yet change my mind.'

It was then that a young servant hurried from an alleyway crying out 'Oh, sir, I am in distress. I know not what to think or say, for they have turned me out of doors.'

James shrank from him. The word now unutterable. 'Ye have the...'

'Nay, sir, I am so far saved, but 'tis the vintner – he is

leaving Town and hath turned me out of doors with not a penny for a wheaten loaf. Ye are a man of God,' he cried, clutching at the priest, 'Tell me what to do.'

'I – I know not.' Suddenly the priest's faith deserted him and for a moment he floated in a vague dystopia, losing all trust in his God. The doctor intervened.

'Perchance apply to the magistrate for relief, and they do offer alms in the parish,' he told the boy. He turned to James: 'Stay within thyself and think, sir. If ye intend to go, then go ye now. Yet mark thy Master, the bravest of us all, and ye will stay.'

'I mark Him, though I am afeared,' said James.

'Then, for the sake of Jesus Christ, help this poor boy to the magistrate for alms – or to thy church for sustenance.'

'For the Lord Jesus Christ, I shall,' said James, making the sign of the cross. 'Come hither, boy.'

'Ah, 'tis well, for we have need of thee,' sighed the doctor. 'The list shall multiply, and daily more able-bodied and wealthy merchants prepare to leave – yet all but saints do take their servants with them.'

And the poor boy looked up at them with quivering lips – a tear in each eye.

12

Who would have believed that Jack Hogg could be of use? While some poor souls laboured at the filthiest jobs in town – cleaning effluent, digging graves… he carelessly swept the inn-yard, hoping to slope off to a gaming house or cock-fight if the opportunity arose; but all public gatherings, except for twice daily services at the parish church, were banned lest they should spread the plague. Jack Hogg harboured a grudge, for it was scarcely possible to cut a purse now.

One afternoon, fancying he heard tell of an illicit game nearby, Jack leant on his besom and beckoned a fellow gambler, whispering in his rasping tones: 'Alf – Alfred! There be a cock-fight down Shoe Lane.'

But the inn-keeper, overhearing his plan, said: 'Cock-fight? Nay, 'tis closed – so too is it all. Get and clean the rubbish lest I fetch the constable. The horn did blow and 'tis the raker coming.'

'Pooh!' spat Jack, watching the inn-keeper out of sight and pretending to sweep.

'Speak ye?' queried Alf, limping over.

'Deaf and lame!' barked Jack, repeating slowly and deliberately: 'I-said-there-be-a-cock-fight-down-Shoe-Lane.'

'Nay, the constable hath moved the rogues on.'

'Moved them on? Bah! The tippling house all shut up, and all for few blotches and purples.'

'Ay, and the playhouses long since, and they do say…'

'A plague on the bastards,' raved Jack, throwing his broom at Alf as though poor Alf, and only Alf – was responsible for the plague and every attendant ill on earth. 'I'll not stand for 't and there's the truth.' He swivelled round: 'What's the mischief?'

'Bess be here, 'tis Bess,' said Alf.

'I see the drab.'

'Jack, Jack, have ye seen my pennies?' she asked urgently.

Jack's shifty eyes told all. 'Pennies?'

'Ay, I did put the pennies in a pot by the casement and 'tis empty – but 'tis Jim,' she said desperately, 'he be sick, Jack, and the doctor did tell me to make a posset. He wants things, Jack.'

'Wants or needs?' Jack continued to sweep, lazily.

'Do not tarry, Jack.'

'Tarry, tarry?'

'We need ye. Please find my pennies.'

'Our pennies, our money. What's mine be mine and what's yours be mine too.' He threw his head back and was laughing long when the inn-keeper called urgently.

'Bess, ye must come hither – before 'tis too late.'

'No, oh, no!' she cried, and made haste to the inn.

Jack watched her go. 'What is 't? – Ah, 'tis well to keep away from the drab.'

'Eh?' said Alf, adjusting his ear.

Christ, ye deaf bastard!' spat Jack with contempt, and shouted: 'I said we'll to the bear-baiting.'

'Nay, there be no cock-fighting, Jack, 'tis closed.'

'I said bear-baiting! I could as well talk to myself.' He turned. 'What's that, wench?' he asked, seeing Bess return in distress.

'No! Dear God, no, 'tis little Jim!' she cried from the

depths of her soul. 'He be taken, Jack.'

'What?'

'He be taken and 'tis Heaven's lucky day.'

She reached out to him but he thrust her aside. 'Ye will not pass the vapours.'

'Just a kind word, Jack, just a kind word.'

She looked up at him, her eyes deep with pleading, her falling tears mixed with the smuts about her face, but Jack looked beyond her tears – only to himself.

'Taken, my boy?'

At this Bess rose up: 'Thy boy, thy boy?' she said wildly. 'Was he thy boy when he did help me all day long in the hovel when I be sick and ye did kick him for 't? Was he thy boy when ye did chide him for his nightmares – aye – and did goad him and beat me for looking to 't? And when, at four years old, he did lose his way in the fields to pick buttercups for me, and I did ramble after him till darkness fell, and all the while ye were merry in the tippling house caring not that I did scream myself hoarse at the fright of it – was he thy boy then? Or at night when he did call out with a painful ear and I did sit with him and soothe him till the cock crowed in the morn? And this woeful day when he did lie abed sweating a fever and I did mop his soaking brow – was he thy boy then? Thy boy? Ye did kick my belly ere he came into the world. "I did never trust a tavern wench" ye said. Ye never even owned that he be thine.' She quietened. 'Ye never gave him an ounce of love, Jack.' And sinking down she said bitterly: 'Now he shall never be thy boy.'

The doctor found her sobbing on the ground and

stooped down to her. 'Bess, Bess – Oh, dear Lord, 'tis the tokens! Poor girl, poor sorry girl.' Picking her up, he turned to Jack Hogg: 'Did thou never call her by her name?'

Jack bristled. 'Life's a bastard to me, 'tis a bastard. Ye are all against Jack Hogg!'

It was then that Alfred, with misguided loyalty, limped up and put his hand on Jack's arm. 'Thou wilt be better for a warm ale, Jack.'

The doctor could no longer look upon Jack's grizzled face. 'Come, poor Bess. Oh, 'tis a long while since I have seen a more woeful day.'

13

To imagine the death of Bess and her little boy, Jim, is to remember that there were tragedies like theirs around every corner in 1665. This was the real human cost, and the thought should bring tears to the eyes. Moreover, questions are bound to be asked. Why did some citizens – good and bad alike – die in abject distress, while others walked free from the plague? Surely it had been potent enough to rid the city of its entire population. Yet amid the filth, the choking air and riot of contamination, citizens of diverse character escaped 'God's infinite wrath'. They say that the diarist, Samuel Pepys, who chronicled much of the plague, survived because of his good humour. Perhaps that, after all is said and done, it comes to just that: a state of mind. An overplus of despair has never assisted the human condition. For Samuel and Mopsa – they didn't despair long…

'This is hell on earth, I cannot bear it!'

'What ails, ye Mopsa?'

'What ails me? Why need ye ask? Do ye not see it all around thee? Poor little Jim Hogg – and now 'tis Bess.'

'Ay, 'tis terrible, Mopsa,' nodded Samuel, unable to comfort her.

'My mistress doth leave town anon. I know not where to go,' she said, pacing about. 'And they did seize the little dog, that ever did follow me around, to kill him.'

'But 'tis for the best.'

The best!' She challenged him 'Nay, 'twas insects

caused the plague – the physician did say.'

'Insects?'

'Ay, the physician doth swear it. Yet they do slaughter, without mercy, hundreds of innocent creatures. I cannot and I shall not aby it!'

'Be comforted,' said Samuel, drawing close.

'Do not touch me!' she exclaimed, moving away.

'Ye are afraid of infection?'

'I am afraid of mine own for thee.'

'I should not come near, for I am afraid of mine own for thee.' He boldly took her by the arm. 'We are, Mopsa, two sides of the same coin. The plague that would take one without the other were crueller still.'

'It takes the whole coin or naught!' she laughed.

'Naught would be best,' and they laughed together.

'We laugh,' said Mopsa, her smile fading. 'My father and brother, your sister and uncle – the shoemaker gone and we do laugh. All of London Town doth breathe with one distempered breath. We do douse ourselves in vinegar and drink plague-water. How long till you and I be taken with tokens to be locked in the pest-house? How long before we take our last fatal breath and they do shovel us, without a song, in to the plague-pit?'

'Ah, 'tis bad for us both. I have inherited a shoemaker's shop, but nobody bothers about shoes today. The rich who would buy them, with all their bows, have left the city and the afflicted do not desire them.'

'Nay.'

'What say ye? My other uncle keeps a forge in Norfolk.' He withdrew a coin from his purse. 'Heads or tails?'

'What trick is this?'

'Heads we go,' but the coin he tossed landed on tails. Suddenly he heard a whimpering nearby, 'and tails we take him with us!'

'Look, 'tis my little dog, he hath escaped!' cried Mopsa.

'Hush!' warned Samuel. 'They would take him if they could. Pray God he doth not bark. We must hide him in a basket when we leave.'

Enfolding the little dog in her apron, Mopsa shed a tear. 'Thank the dear Lord he hath escaped. Now we durst not stay.'

'Nay. We will go early on the morrow – but yet we do need bills of health. We must to the Lord Mayor's office while we are yet well.'

'But 'tis dangerous,' said Mopsa warily. 'They do say the highway is blocked and they do attack strangers.'

'No matter what ye have heard, for 'tis word of mouth – Jack Hogg's – and would ye trust the word of a stinkard? I have my uncle's army tent. We shall bide our time, sleep in the fields and make our way to Norfolk. Anon we shall decide which road to take. Ah, 'tis the priest – in friendlier countenance.'

'Good morrow, friends.'

'Good morrow, sir.'

'Tell me, have ye seen aught of the family, Fitzgibbon?'

'I have not. Perchance Mopsa hath seen them?'

'Ay, they did leave, but 'tis hard to find them now. The coaches and horses and people do crowd together in Drury Lane.'

'I have heard thus,' said James, 'and clumsy coaches caught wheel on wheel. Do ye leave London Town?'

'We shall get our provisions and be gone erewhile,' said Samuel.

'Then, good luck to ye, my friends – and may the good Lord go with thee.'

'We thank thee, sir,' said Mopsa. 'Do ye stay?'

'Ay, for the coward I am.'

'Nay,' said Mopsa, 'for 'tis brave to stay. I have watched thee counselling thy flock. Fare thee well, sir.'

'Fare thee well.'

So, Jessica had gone. James knew well he was selfish to want her to stay in the smoke and the filth with the stench of death and among the weeping and the cries of despair, but he wanted her there. God forgive him as the sinner he tried not to be, but he wanted her there!

On his return to the church, he glanced at her garden gate. He imagined for a moment that he heard the rustle of silk and saw her half-turn to look at him. But there was nothing there but the morning mist and the cluster of wild rose-buds growing into the lane. One of them had burst, and a pink petal – that was all – had opened out. The rest were still tightly bound. They would blossom soon, he thought, for Midsummer was well on its way.

14

So it was that while many lay dying of the plague, those who were able to do so attempted to leave London, either to make their way to other towns and cities or to camp in the fields until the visitation was over. London, a trading capital of the world, was densely populated at that time, and it is not hard to imagine the chaos; the pushing, the shoving of those on foot, the crude carts and clumsy coaches caught edge to edge, a tailback of weary refugees from the city in search of cleaner air, many with no idea where they were going or how. Neither is it hard to imagine the hostility of neighbouring towns that could not countenance an influx of Londoners, many of whom were suspected of carrying with them the plague, as, indeed, many of them did. As in all times of crises, there was a proliferation of violence. Some travellers were threatened with weapons or robbed for the little they had. Others were turned away from shops or made to drop their coins in pots of vinegar, lest they should spread the infection. For many souls in despair, outside London, there could be no place of refuge.

And what of the fates of those who were imprisoned in their own homes? It has been said that some citizens, who had been locked up unjustly in an infected house, fiddled the locks from inside and simply walked out of the door, others clambered over the rooftops to safety – each carrying a bundle and setting out on the treacherous road to freedom. No doubt, as human nature was not always a stranger to compassion, some of the exiles from the city found a safe haven and hoped to return to London Town in healthier times. But for those left behind, there seemed no end to the squalid conditions of plague, and such as the doctor and priest – were caught up in the ill-whirl of a misery-go-round.

Lord Mayor, aldermen, magistrates, constables, watchmen... The chain of command surely disintegrated as the plague claimed more and more lives – although the Lord Mayor held on. In high and low places many were carried off, others were weighed too heavily on or scared out of their wits. Indeed, it was recorded that some citizens died of fright. All this was fecund soil for the lawless, and no soil at all for the poor and vulnerable.

For the likes of Doll and Alf, it would not be long before they, too, were shovelled without ceremony into the plague pit. A few weeks beforehand, hapless Doll would have been incarcerated with a sick family with the threat of never seeing daylight again, but now that the plague came on apace, there were few watchmen to guard the houses – the inmates using their wiles to move about as they pleased. Doll was not without cunning. Cunning was something that she had cultivated since she was a young scullery maid in a prominent Puritan household during the civil war. Painful moral strictures imposed on her during that pious time, rankled. Naturally, after the King had ridden back into London to great jubilation and her employers had hastened from home, Doll was ready to be reconciled to sin.

Poor old Alf had been pressed into Cromwell's army

during the civil war, where he had been deafened courtesy of cannon-shot, and lamed courtesy of the sword. Used and tipped back into society after the Restoration, with no recourse to army rations, he had found himself destitute, until the kindly inn-keeper found him a lowly job in return for a bite to eat and a bed in the hayloft. Alf had been God-fearing once and had no wiles of his own but found it needful to follow others, whomsoever those others might be. The pity was, that he was destined to follow the likes of Doll and Jack Hogg.

Hundreds, on the edge of humanity like Doll and Alf, complete with their own – often tragic stories, found themselves knee-deep in the muck and filth of life. Sadly, for them and those like them, they were destined to sink in the mire of the plague.

'Doll! Doll!' cried Alf, 'They be shutting up houses, Doll.'

'What's that?'

'Have ye got mine ears? I said they be shutting up houses.'

'Ay, that I know.' She coughed into the – already filthy – air and continued sweeping. 'And they be shutting me up along with them.'

'Eh? What, Doll?'

'They've took me for nurse-keeper.'

'Nurse-keeper,' repeated Alf, struggling closer. 'What be that?'

'To nurse the sick and clean up after the devils – 'tis a filthy job. I'll be in for a month o' Sundays.'

'Pooh, the vapours!' exclaimed Alf.

'Ay, the stench. But 'tis only to live, Alf.'

'We must all of us live,' he agreed, 'and 'tis good ye got work, Doll, but what about me? No work for me when the inn be shut.'

'Nay, 'twas Providence, Alf. They do want the wretches left behind to do the dirty work.'

'Ay, the sexton doth want workers for the pits. I'll to him. Bah, 'tis a bastard. To work, Doll.' He jumped to a dig in the rump: 'Constable!'

'Clear that rubbish along there. The raker be blowing his horn. Where be Jack Hogg?'

'Why, what hath he done?'

'Done – 'tis more what he hath not done. Where be the villain?'

'Up in the hayloft smoking his pipe.'

'Smoking? There be hell-fires enough,' snapped the constable, sniffing the fuggy air. 'Tell the oaf he's wanted for the dead carts.'

'Dead carts? Ay, that'll keep him out o' trouble. Do there be aught for me?'

'Ay, to stop a mischief – there be jobs aplenty. Come my way, Alf. But first, I'll pull him down from there. Jack Hogg!' he bawled.

'We've got to live, eh, Doll?' said Alf.

'Ay,' she said, 'We've got to live.'

In this manner, the hapless pair chattered on without a thought for their own ill-fate, yet there were citizens who gathered up their possessions and ran forth, bearing their fate very much in mind.

'Mary, hasten to the bakehouse and we'll be gone,' said one, ironically.

'Good even,' said James, chancing upon them, noticing the citizen covering his face.The man did not want to answer but moving suddenly away, murmured, 'Ay.'

'Ye were in my church not long since, and now 'tis a fright for ye to speak?' he queried.

'We be leaving,' the citizen answered at a safe distance.

'Then I shall bid thee safe journey, and may God...'

Suddenly, the citizen sneezed. James stepped away, for the shock of the sneeze had shaken the man senseless. He swayed, his legs failing from under him. It was true that some of the victims, like this unfortunate fellow, had few symptoms to begin with and hardly realised that they had caught the infection – then came a sneeze, the dreaded precursor to the plague, and blood ran cold before it boiled, for they knew they would be taken well before the week was out. They still believed that it was possible to be frightened to death, and cases were recorded. And at this time, fear stalked the streets, the lanes, the alleyways... until there was nowhere to hide.

'Bless ye, sir,' said James, carefully approaching. 'Ye have a bill of health, I do presume?'

The citizen ignored the question, calling: 'Mary! Mary! Phew...I do feel...'

'Stand away, he doth collapse,' said James in anguish. 'Oh, Heaven's mercy, 'tis another. Doctor!'

'I cannot stay, I am called to the bakehouse,' put in the doctor, urgently. 'Oh, sweet Lord, 'tis another with the tokens. I would I had a goodly nurse-keeper. Help, me, James!'

Catching sight of the sweat and blotches upon the citizen, James dithered, but the doctor thrust an open bottle under his nose: 'Drink this.'

'Nay.'

'Drink it, I say,' he insisted, 'that ye may souse the vapours.'

'I thank thee,' said James, choking it back.

'Good, 'tis an evil will protect ye,' said the doctor. 'Now, through Duck Alley – close by stands his house. This poor soul will not be leaving London by coach, I fear,' he said beneath his breath, 'but by cart.'

'I do bethink me, the daughter is at the bakehouse,' said James.

'Nay, the plague doth go before her,' said the doctor, willing the afflicted citizen along.

'Oh, the Lord Christ, protect us!' James followed.

15

The next few days saw an upsurge of citizens leaving London Town. Chests, cases, hatboxes – all piled onto coaches and carts as frightened citizens prepared to flee the devilish distemper. Some hastened to the apothecary for cures or to the Exchange, others hurried to the grocer or bakehouse with a list of provisions – if they could be had. A good number of butchers and other suppliers had already died of the plague, leaving the bulks and stalls, such as the shoemaker's and cobbler's, abandoned or locked up.

Samuel and Mopsa were among the throng on foot with a hand-cart containing provisions, the tools of a shoemaker's trade and, hidden in a basket with a tent on top, the only little dog left in London Town. The doctor didn't notice them as they trundled on amid so many anxious souls on the move.

'Chaos! First my physic,' he said, fortifying himself, 'and now – Ah, James, it seems I have another charge – Anon, I come!'

James watched his friend hurry through the stone archway and up the alley. He looked around him. No longer did he want to run away but was impelled to fight on, to stay safe to beat the plague. As the fleeing crowds rolled into the distance like the passing of a storm, he stood aside and mused a moment about how he would come through this nightmare and wake up in the light, find a peaceful country church and settle down. Yet however hard he tried he barely had the strength, for he was completely enervated. He looked up, ashen-faced, and asked himself: 'What kind of God is mine?'

Suddenly, a voice seemed to float down from a cloud. 'Sir!'

It came again, imperiously. 'Sir!'

'Jessica, I...'

'What ails thee, my pious friend?'

'Naught ails me, but that I am spent – But why dost thou ask?'

'For that ye did look distracted, and 'tis a time so dark that I do fear for all my friends.'

'Ye fear for me, Jessica? Even for one as pious as I?'

'Even for one as pious as thee,' she said with unwonted tenderness.

He blushed– the devil! Her unexpected presence made him blush. He collected himself: 'I thank thee for that, lady. Tell me, how came ye here? When ye were not at church, I believed ye had gone to Huntingdon betimes.'

'How did ye notice in a crowded church?'

'The congregation, that but a week hence was filled with repenting souls, now dwindles by the hour, for they all leave, by coach or through the door of death. All but a poor few do lock themselves in pews, apart, and pray.'

'Poor souls,' she sighed.

'Ay, but I am glad they pray. When do ye go to Huntingdon?'

'We go on the morrow, after my father hath attended to business matters. Oh, dear, see the sundial. It is getting late and there is so much to be done – so many dresses still to pack.'

'Ay – but I am sad to see ye go. Methought ye

intended to stay, and for that – the selfish fool I am – was glad.'

'I would be happy to stay but cannot. I am but twenty years and a little more – in age, and in my father's charge.'

'True, 'tis true ye must not stay. It was a selfish thought, because – Go safely Jessica.'

'Before I go...' She offered to kiss him but drew suddenly away. 'Oh, nay, I must not kiss thee in the mist of vapours.'

'Kiss me?'

'Oh, sir, ye blush!'

'Nay, I do not.' He shifted about uneasily. Again, he had blushed in her presence.

'Ye are...'

'Yes, what am I?'

'A torment.'

She remained for a moment, twisting a nosegay of rue beneath her chin, and added: 'Yet I would kiss ye if I could.' With a teasing smile she turned to go, but turning back, said in serious tones: 'Wear this for me. It is of the gentle Jesus.' She pressed her cross in his hand. 'I shall be safe erewhile and have no need of it. I bid thee wear it. Fare thee well, priest.' With a sinking heart he watched her step away, and called: 'Farewell, dear lady.'

'Then I am not a torment?'

'That shall remain in question,' he said, watching her go.

In a moment she was on her way, remembering that he had blushed. The pious priest had blushed. 'Wherefore? Ah, good to look upon and sensitive. It shows he somewhere hath a heart,' she thought, 'and I shall claim it by-and-by.' She smiled, dimpling her cheek. 'I shall write that in my diary!'

It was true James was Puritan. He once had no choice, for he was brought up in a God-fearing family, shunning all excesses in a world without emotion, without fun. It was a grey life, circumscribed by the strictures of puritanism which had prevailed for eighteen years. In 1660, he had stood in the street with thousands of other citizens and watched King Charles II ride into London on a white horse leading a great procession. The streets were festooned with flags and bunting, bells rang out and the people cheered. Suddenly the whole of London Town had burst with bows, feathers, glitter and colour to welcome the monarch home. As a young man, James had never seen anything like it and, throwing aside the puritanical yoke, stood cheering in the crowd that welcomed the King – until his father pulled him away by the collar and boxed his ears.

Soon after the King returned triumphantly to be re-united with the throne, the Puritan clergy were expelled from the Church of England and, dissenters in order with the Act of Uniformity in 1662, were made to swear allegiance to the King and adopt the Book of Common Prayer. But this did not apply to James who had lately chosen to be ordained in the Church of England. Nonetheless, much of the old Puritan piety still clung to him.

James had never had a deep conversation with a woman before, and certainly had never been kissed by one. Now his blood was hot and he stood trembling. He didn't notice the doctor come upon him from the alley.

'Still with us, James?'

He did not answer at first, for his mind was still with Jessica. 'Ay,' he said at length, 'yet I should be gone a long while hence – safe in Huntingdon – 'twere not for thee.'

'What mean ye, sir?'

'Ye bid me stay to comfort my flock. Wherefore? I have no flock – only death, disease, disaster and the chaos of hell. I thank thee not.'

'Ye thank me not?' The doctor was stunned at the affront. He grew first florid, then purple with rage: 'A fig! Ye are, I trust, master of thine own conscience? Ye crow enough about the sins of others, sir, yet offer thine own sins with impunity. Thou art a hypocrite and I bid thee good day!'

'Nay, doctor,' said James, putting a hand on his friend's shoulder, 'do not go, for 'tis the truth ye speak. I am the worst of hypocrites. I do repent me and beg thy forgiveness.' His entire body deflated now: 'I am spent, doctor, spent...'

'So too are we all,' said the doctor. 'I have dressed wounds, let blood, incised the buboes – though some of them are so hard, they will not bear the slicing of them – and ye stand lily-livered and love-struck. This is the backcloth of a tragedy and we must ride out the dark clouds ere we may see the sun.' The doctor sighed long and hard: 'Sit ye down, friend. Come share my wheaten bread and cheese and drink the physic.' He sighed. 'I do but stop for sustenance.'

'I thank thee, 'tis long since I have eaten,' said James.

'And I. My cook hath gone – I know not where. She left no victuals – the pantry's bare. She took the victuals with her, I'll be bound. Methinks she fled to the fields. But 'tis a goodly feast. It was my good fortune to get it from a grateful alderman that once I helped,' he said, washing it down with a swig. He smacked his lips. 'Tell me, James, what of the lady Jessica, for she hath put ye in a fit?'

'She hath gone forth to Huntingdon – and at such a time I love her.'

'Nay, tis ill-advised in the midst of pestilence,' said the doctor.

'This I do know.' The whisky coursing through his veins, James brightened. 'I must resolve to comfort the few weary souls I can.'

'Ay, James. Those who are not carried away with plague are carried away from London if they durst. The highway is blocked – so too the lanes – and the villagers are afeared of the contagion coming their way. Though God knows I do not blame them.'

'Ay, 'tis an exodus and they are much affrighted,' agreed James.

As they sat and ate, a crowd of citizens gathered in the square, perplexed and disorganised, looking here and there, each wary of the other's breath. One, a cloth merchant, had been known to bully his servants when the mood took him. And the mood took him now.

'Fare ye well,' he barked. 'I do not choose – but there is no room for ye, so go thy ways and shift for thyself.'

'Whither?'

'Where thou list.'

The servant walked disconsolately away, looking back over his shoulder as though hoping for a reprieve.

'Get thee gone!' shouted the merchant. At once, aware of the doctor's censure, he edged nearer – though at a safe distance. 'Ye sit, doctor – passing the time of the day and tippling for thyself? Why dost thou sit when so many have need of thee?'

James rose up. 'For that the doctor hath not dined for four and twenty hours.'

'For that I do beg pardon,' said the odious citizen, continuing to give orders. 'Take the hat boxes, Elizabeth, and take t' other side of the trunk, John. I said t 'other side, lad, t' other side!'

'Nay, 'tis too heavy,' complained his wiry son.

'Where be the servant?' The cloth merchant stalked about in mock despair, spitting oaths. 'Where be the servant? Jacob! Jacob, come hither!'

But Jacob would not. 'Nay, I go my ways,' he said, 'for ye have turned me out.'

The bully would have boxed his ears if he could catch him, but the servant dodged behind the carts and coaches out of sight. The merchant turned to James: 'Priest!' he called, 'Ye know me to be virtuous...'

'I know ye but not thy virtues,' said James. 'Yet I shall be glad to help ye out of town – with my boot,' he said beneath his breath, astounded at the change that was coming upon him. Then, grabbing the other end of the trunk, he helped heft it onto a coach. Soon, with the neigh of a horse and a rattle of hooves it was gone.

James watched it out of sight. 'Doctor, I lose my

propriety,' he said, adding with an edge of contempt: 'I fain would have shown him my boot.'

I am glad to see some spirit in thee at last!' laughed the doctor. 'But I tarry, and must to the College. Now they do say the effluvium creeps up from the earth, and we must discuss the facts, for I do believe it came down to the earth from the comet.'

'From the sky or up from the earth, 'tis all one,' said James, 'for surely it hath come from God. I must to the church to pray.'

16

The King and his court were in Oxford, leaving London in the capable hands of Sir John Lawrence, the Lord Mayor – supported by the magistrates, justices, aldermen and common councillors. To begin with, law and order was well maintained by the constables and watchmen, but with so many citizens dead, dying or fled – including those designated to keep the peace, the Lord Mayor was becoming overwhelmed by the scale of the disaster. Moreover, a great number of clergymen, physicians, apothecaries and other citizens, had left the city – leaving a few dedicated souls, brave enough to remain, to cope alone. Public order was beginning to break down, and disorder destined to supervene. A good deal of those left in London – so sadly called the 'useless mouths' – were too poor to leave, and often had nowhere to turn but to the parish for alms; but the rogues, intent on exploiting any situation for a penny, together with a number of ghoulish necromancers, flourished. It was as though the devil whispered in their ears 'Rats may play...' and rats – including the likes of Jack Hogg – carried fleas. Thus, in the heat of the summer of 1665, the plague raged on...

'How now, doctor. How goes it with Sir John?'

The doctor paused and shook his head gravely, indicating that the Lord Mayor was in an unenviable position. There were not enough officers to enforce the law now that the plague carried the citizens away in such alarming numbers. Bodies were beginning to pile up on the streets, on the stairs, and even floated down the

Thames – strewing the city with sights that were dreadful to behold.

'He no longer knows what to do or say – such is his conundrum. They say he thinks it imprudent to lock up houses now, for it is a measure that yields more deaths than may be saved. Yet 'tis the policy.'

'I have heard the King sends alms for the poor. Is it so?' asked James.

'Ay, 'tis so. The magistrate – the sot with the crooked periwig – doth unlock his jaw when he be merry and liberates the news betimes. His Majesty hath sent a sum of one thousand pounds for the relief of the poor.'

'One thousand pounds?'

'Ay, to be distributed in four parishes. And daily the Lord Mayor gives alms, for the rich do follow the King in his benevolence and do fill the coffers.'

'Yet still some poor souls know not whither to go and chaos rules, for London Town is overwhelmed,' said James in concern.

'Ay. But by the grace of God, there are still angels in our midst,' said the doctor.

'And demons, too, I see,' said James, noting his friend indulging in his accustomed tipple.

'Other poor souls do incarcerate themselves for fear of taking the infected air. Thus, do they spread the vapours all about them in their homes. The physicians say 'tis ill-wisdom, for either way the vapours spread, but yet there may be some relief for us if the miasma doth blow with the wind towards the east of London Town. Be not so sure and mark me – the plague will not abate until the frost.'

'The devil!'

'Ay, the fiend is in his element. Oh, if ye saw the nurse-keepers they employ – filthy, rough, they care not for a fig – the likes of Doll.'

'Nay, surely not!'

'Ay, the owner of that gummy, one-tooth mouth that doth exhale more stinking breath than all the plague. The garlic that she chews upon all day doth make it sail forth tenfold on the air.' He paused for another tipple. 'Forgive my lack of charity.'

'Ye are absolved, 'tis foul. Are there no gentlefolk to nurse the sick?'

'All going thither – or taken with the plague, and 'tis more than hell on earth. Would that I had one gentle soul – unafraid to work – than all this motley crew. Bring me a catholic nun, James.'

'A catholic nun? Surely 'tis popery!'

'Yet they can do the work.'

'But to ensure a seat in Heaven,' objected James. 'The Church doth say that they do seek favour with the Lord by ministering to the sick for that they would improve their souls.'

'I care not that they seek favour with the Lord,' argued the doctor. 'It is better than seeking favour with the devil.'

'Ye are wise, doctor, for there are miscreants abroad.'

'Ay, and to compound our woes, now that the inn is infected, 'tis Jack Hogg rides the dead-cart!'

'Nay!'

'See, James – still they go forth.'

'Ay. I see the journeyman is leaving town. I hope 'tis

not to Huntingdon. Good even sir,' said James, approaching him. 'We have met before.'

'I do remember thy piety.'

'I am a priest, sir, and 'tis my work to be pious.'

'Ye did exceed the expectations of thy office, sir,' said the journeyman.

'I do apologise, for my zeal, sir.' Conversation came easily now that he supposed Jessica to have no interest in the man. 'Ye work for the silk-merchant, Fitzgibbon, do ye not?'

'Nay, I work for him no more.'

'Saw ye his family before they left?'

'I did not. He hath left me to go my ways. It is well for him, for his uncle is a lord and his family rich. I go the way of all abandoned journeymen and take my chances for a crust.'

'Whither?'

'Perchance to Oxford for a while, close by where the King doth lodge. I still have silk and ribands good to sell, but 'tis certain they need not fripperies in London Town. I would do better to trade in winding sheets.'

'For that I am truly sorry,' said James, offering him a shilling.

'I thank ye – but his daughter did give me a purse before I went on my way,' said the journeyman.

'His daughter gave thee a purse?'

'Ay, the lovely Jessica.'

'Ye must not talk thus!' said James.

The journeyman continued to spill his information freely in James's ear. 'She is a goodly soul, and I did hope...'

'Hope?'

'That she would take me for her beau.'

'Then ye may continue to hope, sir,' said James, suppressing his anger, 'for methinks the lady already hath a beau.'

'Ay, she did tell me she hath a secret beau. I wonder who he be, for I fain would skewer him,' and he accompanied his bravado with the swish of an imaginary sword. It was well he turned to busy himself with a bundle of dropped ribands, for James clenched his fist in a passion, and said: 'Thy coach is leaving, sir!'

'Sam! Sam!' called the journeyman, 'On board if ye be coming. A tangle of horses and carts shall block the road. Farewell, priest,' he said, too busy to witness the priest's anxiety.

'More families go their ways,' said the doctor. 'What is it, James? Ye are distracted.'

'She did tell him!'

'Eh – What mean thee – tell him?'

'The lady Jessica did tell the journeyman she had a secret beau. How so? I am perplexed, doctor – for I know not if that secret beau be me!'

The doctor laughed. 'The lady Jessica confounds thy senses, James. Nay – I must not laugh. I see no end to woes – yet 'tis my nature to be merry. Ah, I see friends. They take the coach. Good even...'

The gentleman stood aloof: 'Fare thee well, sir. Do not come near. Ye parley with the afflicted.'

'Parley with the afflicted?' repeated the doctor, astounded.

'Yes, sir, and I shall have none of it.'

'I do not parley with the afflicted, sir. I do minister to the sick.'

'Nay, 'tis all one,' said the man, 'Step away!' He turned to his wife and daughter: 'Jane, Meg, into the coach.' Covering his mouth with his kerchief, he bundled them in the coach with their belongings and, jumping aloft, bid the coachman drive on.

The doctor stood bewildered, took a sip of whisky, shook the flask hopefully, finished the contents and contemplated that there were shades of bad behaviour: those who would murder the afflicted in their beds – all for a bit of decent linen, those who would rob a corps for a ring, those who would play with the dead or taunt the mourners, those who would manhandle in the name of the law – and sometimes the lesser evil of treating a friend like an enemy.

'I do be sorry to see thee insulted in such a manner,' said James. 'Yet, do not fret, doctor, 'tis the times.'

'The times! I tell thee, that...that... but I shall hold my tongue. Many a time I have done a good turn for that fellow and for his family, and asked not a fig in return, sir, nor a fig leaf in return.'

'Ay, a good turn once done is a favour soon forgotten,' said James.

'I say no more or I shall – I shall – go off like a – a cannon,' said his friend.

James noticed – not for the first time of late – that the doctor was slurring his words. He watched him closely.

'Ah, I see the... tallow chandler goes forth,' he continued, 'I have a friend in him.' He swayed and stepped into the dusty road to hail the chandler. 'Ye leave town, Simon? Whither do ye go?'

But the chandler thrust out the flat of a hand and, with the other, raised his kerchief towards his face. 'Do not come near – a physician is not free of it,' and leaving the doctor staggering, turned away and yelled: 'Matthew – post horses!'

The poor doctor was so shocked by a second affront, that he swayed and, but for James dragging him out of the way, would have gone under the wheels of a cart.

'Doctor! Ye do avoid the plague, yet would be carried away by a cart!'

'I know not what to say,' said the doctor. He shook, then lifting his flask to his mouth, exploded: 'Empty!'

'Ye do drink too much, said James,' shaking his head.

'Yet still I am here. I am here, yet so many are not.' Suddenly, tears flowed and he tried to beat them back: tears for the afflicted, tears for the friends who had forsaken him and, in that moment, tears for all the woes in the world.

'Come, sir, I shall see thee safely home. Ye dress no wounds today,' said James.

17

The sick ran mad about the streets now, shrieking and crying out for the Lord to save them. Moreover, it has been said that some were in such agony from lumps and swellings on their poor bodies that they ended their suffering by plunging into the Thames.

The air was still and hot, and London Town was choking from the night fires lit to purge the filthy air. Few healthy citizens dared to walk the streets and alleyways now. Those who did crept stealthily, masked by kerchiefs, and some sniffed pomades stuffed with sweet-smelling herbs or fragrant posies to ward off the distemper. In such times, when many people still believed in the vengeance of God, and now that death was a reality, they feared Death stalking them with his scythe ready to strike them down. They would hide from him if they could. Yet early up and about this morning were a few careless souls with orders from the Lord Mayor to keep the peace, nurse the sick, or keep the way clear of the corpses that in the heat of summer caused a stench. And the stench was gross indeed. At best, rubbish had accumulated in decomposing heaps, at worst, animal matter and other filth was trampled underfoot while effluence flowed freely from the open sewers and cesspools round about. All the while, the feculent vapours hung heavily in the air – and the devil Plague laughed at the swing of a pomander or wave of a fragrant posy down the street.

The constable lacked patience now…

'Doll!'

'Ay,' she responded, wiping her filthy hands on her apron.

'Are ye appointed nurse-keeper, Doll?'

'Why, 'tis the hour?'

'Ay. The examiner is at the tailor's shop and summons ye.'

The tailor's shop, 'tis visited?'

'Ay.'

'Ah, 'tis certain I'll ne'er see July. Let the devil take them,' she grunted.

'Ah – go thy ways,' said the constable. 'Watchman!'

'Over here.'

'The tailor's shop is to be locked up erelong.'

'Nay, Dan, but his wife be well. Send them the pest-house.'

'There be no room, 'tis overflowed. They must be shut up, Dick.'

'She comes hither, in distress. Ah, 'tis pity, 'tis pity – yet I must do my job,' he said, resolved.

The tailor's wife had heard her fate, but she was young and there was not a blemish on her. Suddenly she ran about distracted, seized with the fear of being locked away with her aged husband and his brother – both sick with fever – for that would be the death of her.

'No, no!' she screamed, 'Do not lock me in! Have ye no pity?'

'Ay, but 'tis orders from the Mayor,' and the watchman clasped her by her tiny arm and dragged her away.

'No, no! Christ have mercy on us!'

'Mark it with a red cross,' ordered the constable, and

be sure to watch outside – two o' ye – d' ye hear?'

'No! No! God in Heaven, no!' cried the tailor's wife – but the heavy door was closed against her and was locked fast.

This ghastly night it was hot, and the fires lit to purify the putrid air flamed as though from hell. A hand-cart rolled along the alley, for the way was too narrow for a horse and cart. Soon it emerged into the street to tip a poor lowly soul, stripped of a winding sheet, into the dead cart. Jack Hogg wheeled the hand-cart, with Alf scurrying in his wake shaking the bell, a bell that clanged a dead sound.

'Ring your bell, Alf,' shouted Jack. 'Bring out your dead! Bring out your dead!' They shouted. The plague had done its worst and the waiting cart bore a heavy load for the horse. 'Watch that overgrown ass! Bring it up close, Alf. Whoa! Steady...Ow! – he kicked me, the jade. I'll show him how to kick all the way to the knackers. Alf, ring the bell.'

Sadly, there are some people who ask what they want from life, not what they can give. Such was Jack Hogg's philosophy. Even in a poor soul's moment of bereavement he was out to make a penny or two. Barely had Death slipped out of the door when he was at it...

'Oi, Alf, grab t' other end,' he rasped, attempting to remove a winding sheet from the newly deceased. 'Naught can he do with it now he be dead. Naked he came into the world, naked he be going out.'

'Yea,' Jack,' said his side-kick, 'a nice bit o' linen.'

'Get ye gone to Martha's house. She be covered in blotches and purples. The old drab got the sneeze. Ay, she be a weak old mare – she'll breathe the last of it, and the devil should carry her off in a nice little winding sheet to keep us in ale.'

'Ay, Jack, 'twill keep us in ale,' chimed Alf, and had himself a drink.

'Give it here!' snapped Jack, grabbing the bottle. 'And keep mum.'

'Oh, ay, I'll keep mum, Jack,' said Alf, for although he was afraid of Jack's brutality, he was more afraid of being left friendless.

At that awful moment, a woman came from the back of a house seeking pity. She was all alone, trying to drag her husband – now lost to her. They say that angels weep, and surely then they did, for the woman was in deep grief and could not countenance parting with him.

'Oh, that he be alive and I be...' she sobbed. From the depths of her belly, she sobbed, and one can only imagine the added despair being heaped upon her when faced with Jack Hogg.

'No use weeping, woman. Let him be. We'll get hold of him. A dead weight!' He complained. 'Drag him, Alf.' They heaved him onto the cart, but the woman stood in the way of the cart and would not let Jack drive it away.

'No, my poor husband. The poor man. He ne'er knew a nasty deed – He ne'er – He – Ye would bury him without a prayer? Is there nobody to hear my sorrow?'

'I hear ye,' said Jack, 'and they all be buried without ceremony.'

'Nay, do not take him yet awhile,' she pleaded.

'Get thee gone to thy house, woman, 'tis the times. Get up – Alf! – Out of the way, woman!'

'God bless thee, my love,' she said. 'Oh, dear God, is there nobody to say a prayer?'

'I shall,' came a voice, strong and determined, emerging from the darkness into the lantern light.

'Priest!' spat Jack.

James did not want the woman to go by the pit-side, for he would save her the horror of it. Making the sign of the cross, he said the Lord's Prayer, for all the victims in the cart, and spoke her husband's name.

'Come ye indoors now,' he told her, and swinging round to Jack said: 'And you can go to hell!'

As James watched the oaf whip the horse away, throwing curses back on the air while the poor woman wept beside him, he knew why he was destined to stay in London Town.

18

Perhaps the roses were afraid to bloom in plague-struck London, for still they remained tightly in bud. Yet roses need rain, and some blamed the dry summer – made worse by the coal fires about the town – for their unwillingness to open. Even now, in summer, blazing fires roared in the grates of houses in a bid to keep the sickness away. It was well for the coal-merchants, for while others languished when their goods were left unsold, they did an excellent trade. The colliers continued to off-load down river, and Newcastle and other towns flourished, unaware of polluting the air and causing discomfort to the dwindling population of London...

The doctor mopped his brow. 'Phew! I long for rain to extinguish the fires. The magistrates say that they do clean the air. I disagree, they do make it filthy. See the smuts upon the wall. What think ye, friend?'

James nodded vaguely.

'The last rush is on, James, for they do close the road. See how the coaches do again gather in a muddle. The horses do neigh and rear for fear, and wheel on wheel, the coaches catch each other they are so close...'

'Ay,' said James.

The doctor turned and looked at him. 'Ha! Talking to myself. Still thinking on the lady Jessica?'

'Nay,' said James.

'Thou shalt not lie, priest,' chuckled the doctor, indulging in a swig. 'Have another, 'twill kill the heinous creatures that do crawl among us.'

'Or make them dance and be merry,' said James.

'Then make them merry,' laughed the doctor, offering up the flask.

'Nay, I thank thee, nay, nay and again I say nay,' said James.

At which the doctor flung back his head and laughed heartily: 'Ha! Ha! A horse ne'er neighed so much. Take care, James – There be a paucity of horses at this hour, and if ye should stand and say *nay* in Drury Lane, they'll mount ye and ride ye to Oxford!'

James waited and, when the joke sank in, joined the doctor in a guffaw that seemed at odds with the weeping around every miserable corner: 'At such a time, I laugh? I ne'er laughed like that before.'

'Ay, 'tis sick, James, 'tis sick, and yet methinks there's something in 't – a potent medicine. Is laughter our saviour at such a time, think ye?'

There came a sudden wail from the alley and an answering scream, as though to remind them of the gravity of the times and chasten them.

The doctor got up. 'Enough of levity. I must be gone.'

'And I,' said James, 'to the little congregation I have. But a month ago, my church was over-filled with penitent souls. I do wonder about the fates of their familiar faces.'

From the far side of the square, James noticed the vintner staggering from his house with a box of wine ready to load it onto a waiting cart. He was off to the country to join his family, for they had travelled ahead some days before. It's strange to say, and nobody knew the reason, that there were some citizens who exhibited neither sign nor symptom of the plague. These citizens were dangerous, for people ate and drank with them, laughed and were merry, heedless of the danger among them. Thus, the vintner who, without knowing it, spread the plague with ease, witnessed many of his friends and associates die all about him. Now came the reckoning. The vintner collapsed, dropping the box of wine before him. Some of the bottles smashed and poured the wine onto the cobbles, others rolled and stopped in the gutter, but the vintner lay there and didn't stir. He was dead.

James hurried over, and saw that the man's eyes were open wide, as though surprised by death, but he could see no tokens or any other sign of the plague, and looked about him for help: 'Constable!'

'Ay?' He came running.

'Come, 'tis the vintner, and he is dead – God rest his soul.'

'Do not touch him,' said the constable, for 'tis the silent plague.'

'What mean ye, "silent plague"?' asked James.

'For there be neither moan nor groan. I'll tell the dead-carters,' he said, and walked away, leaving the vintner semi-prone on the ground, his bottles of wine smashed around him.

James walked away, but looking back, saw that a mean group of citizens had congregated to scavenge the wine. Shaking his head, he smiled wryly and stepped into the lane. As he turned towards the church, he came across an old flower-seller who often put a rose on the altar. She was sitting on the ground by the wall, face hidden in cupped hands, her redundant basket by her side. The woman barely moved and at first James was wary, fearing that she might be plague-struck, but as he passed, she looked up. He could see no tokens, but her wizened face was smudged with tears.

'What ails ye, mistress?' asked James, 'Is thy family carried away with the distemper?'

'Nay sir, I have no family,' she sobbed.'

'Ah, ye live alone so God hath preserved thee,' said James. 'Why, then do ye cry so bitterly from thy soul?'

The woman stood up clasping an empty basket. 'Oh, sir – 'tis the roses, they are afeared.'

'Afeared, mistress? How so – afeared?'

'Afeared for they catch the plague, and not a rose do I have for the church.'

'Do not fret for a rose for the church, for there is so much more to worry us now. For the rose – 'tis the smoke in the air from the fires and the drought hath affrighted their flowers. When God sends rain, and 'twill be soon, they shall do well.'

The old woman seemed comforted by the thought and, with a parting blessing, went slowly back down the lane. James watched her as she lifted the latch of her hovel and let herself in. He chastened himself. He had taken for granted her gifts on the altar, fresh with the changing seasons: the chrysanthemum, the sprig of holly, the daffodil – the rose. What is more, his conscience was uneasy – for he realised that he didn't even know her name. Thinking this, he went wearily towards the church, but before he turned into the churchyard he was minded to stop across the way.

'Jessica's garden, 'tis her garden,' he sighed. It was then that he noticed the musk roses still tightly wrapped in bud as though in fear. It was past Midsummer and not one of them had flowered. Had God turned against nature? It was then that a blackbird whistled suddenly, symbolically on a higher bough as though answering his question.

The song was so clear and so beautiful that it came to him like a revelation. On and on it sang, rising notes above the distant cacophony of the town and the dissonant wailing beside the gaping pit close to the church. James stood listening to the bird and traced it to a nearby elderberry tree. 'That bird is more devout than I!' he thought. He looked to the sky, and stood there for some while, imbibing the peace, until the evening sun burst in all its glory and lit the clouds. He had had his nose to the ground and had never noticed the song of a bird or the beauty of the sunset before. As he approached the lynch-gate, he affirmed what he had thought for some time. It was Jessica who had shown him the way to truth, for he had been praying to the wrong kind of God. He opened the heavy door and went into the church – where knelt a solitary child in prayer.

19

The following evening, after James had led a small group of worshippers in prayer, the old woman from the hovel down the lane ran into the church beside herself – crying out in fear. 'Sir, sir, 'tis the vapours that kill the roses. I tell thee, the plague be killing the world – tis the vapours,' she cried, clutching at him.

James tried to comfort her while she waved her arms, distracted. 'Nay, calm ye down. It cannot last forever. God willing, soon it will be gone, and...'

'Yea, gone, 'twill be gone, and the world will be no more!' She staggered to the altar and with a cry of pain fell down. James recoiled although, seeing neither tokens upon her nor any sign of fever, he hurried to the doctor for help. When they arrived at the church, she was quite still.

'Her heart hath stopped,' said the doctor. 'But 'twas not the distemper that stopped it, for it was tired and could no longer beat. Ye may be sure her death will be entered on the Bill of Mortality, yet it shall not record the plague. E'en so, 'twas the evil plague that distracted her and made her breathe her last.'

'For that I am sorry,' said James. 'Yet we should be thankful for the good Lord's mercy, for she did not suffer – as suffer the poor people must when taken with plague.'

James gently laid the old woman flat, crossed her arms over her chest and, kneeling down beside her, said a prayer. 'There is little room for burial in the churchyard now, but I am loth to stand by while they shovel this goodly woman into the pit, for long hath she said a prayer in my church, and 'tis my shame that never did I ask her name. To make amends: there is yet a corner between the yew tree and the wall. I shall tell the sexton to bid them bury her there.'

'Ay, James, 'tis good. There are many citizens on the bill that die by other means. We do forget other illnesses that do carry people off – so overwhelmed are we by thoughts of the plague.'

'Ay, I had not bethought me,' said James, 'for now I see only one kind of death – one born of the distemper.'

'Witness this. A councillor was taken with an apoplectic seizure a week gone, and other disasters do befall the citizens unaware. My neighbour did take henbane – the stinking nightshade – for that he thought it would protect him, but 'tis poison, James, 'tis deadly poison, and the citizen did not last long.'

'Horrible!'

'The wheelwright did fall under a coach and was killed – so heavy was the muddle   by the city gates – and an alderman did choke upon an onion that he chewed to keep away the vapours. Let there be no doubt that the plague lurked in all these deaths, James – so subtly – that it did not get the blame.'

'The devil!'

'Ay, 'tis the devil.'

The doctor offered James a sip of his good whisky.

'Nay,' said James. 'And for thee – take heed ye do not kill thyself subtly because of the plague!'

The doctor chuckled and swigged it back.

'I'll walk some way to the market square with ye,' said

James, 'for I have need of victuals and no longer have a servant. Of wheaten loaves there are plenty at the bakehouse.'

'Ay,' said the doctor, 'the Lord Mayor doth see to that.'

At the end of the lane where it tuned towards the bakehouse, James stopped for he felt a distinct drip on his hand. Another fell, then another... Suddenly the sky darkened and there was a rumble of thunder. In moments the rain was pelting down at a good rate and they hurried for cover beneath a thatch in the square. Down came the welcome rain, pouring off the rooftops, soaking the thatches, gushing rapidly down into water butts... A few citizens came out of their homes to stand under it and praise God – for this was a great relief in the midst of their woes.

'Bless me!' exclaimed the doctor. 'No cloak and hat – and my periwig soaked.'

James put out his hands to catch the rain. 'Praise the Lord!' he cried, 'See the fires, doctor, they do go out! The rain doth put them out!'

The flaming cressets lodged in the walls of buildings flamed no more, and what remained of the glowing coals in the metal fire-pits hissed, steamed and went out. And all across the plague-hit city, other unwelcome fires spluttered and were no more.

'Ay, it hath extinguished the fires! It is a joyful moment, for I did not approve the practice,' said the doctor. 'Come and sup with me James and we will drink to that, for ye be soaked to the skin and still the sky darkens.' They hurried through the archway towards the doctor's house.

A lantern lit across the way, and Doll appeared suddenly, like a squirming creature flushed out from a hole.

'See how the rain doth seek them out,' said James.

'Ay, the gummy nurse-keeper means no good. She hath left her charges,' said the doctor, 'yet if I were one of her charges, I would be glad of that.'

Doll looked furtively, this way and that and set eyes on the doctor.

He hailed her and approached. 'Why do ye walk abroad spreading the vapours? I bid thee care for Martha till the good Lord carries her away.'

'I do but come to take the air. It doth stink in there,' sniffed Doll, wiping he nose with the back of her hand.

'Ye have taken the air. Now nurse the woman as I bid ye do. Do ye not see, James, why I do crave a goodly soul to nurse the sick?'

'Aye, doctor. I do fear for the sick in such careless hands.'

Doll, muttering curses, went back to Martha's house.

'Yet I do not blame the wretch for wanting air, for 'tis fresher since the rain,' continued James. 'Perchance the vapours have been washed away into the drains.'

'For what the drains are worth, and that is little,' answered the doctor, 'Nay, I do feel it. The miasma still doth hang malignly in the air. Come James, into my house – my palate craves another drink.'

'And my stomach – bread and cheese,' said James.

In conversation, they hadn't noticed the sad scene

that was unfolding nearby, for both priest and physician had not only been saturated by the rain but, in recent days, by the heavy burden of charity pressed upon them. True to say, it was not with indifference that they went inside the house and closed the door.

Nearby, a few poor souls, turned out of doors by their employers, were clustered under the archway to keep dry. They would have sought alms from the mayor had they the strength. Some moaned and some cried, while some – including a sick child – clung to a vestige of life. The child, who cried loudly for a while, sighed away her final breath and it was taken up by the sound of prayers and pitiful wailing. Then all went deathly quiet.

For a while, there was an unusual peace along the rain-soaked streets and alleys, together with new freshness in the air. After the clouds had flung down the last of their burden, windows began to open and people peered out. Some came to the threshold and inhaled the air as though breathing in a cure.

By nightfall, more dead citizens had been deposited in the street awaiting the cart, and Doll sat by a wall, lantern in hand with Martha's poor body propped up beside her. A beam of light from the lantern danced in the darkness and alighted on Martha's hand. Doll smiled a ghastly smile, and her eyes lit up as she caught sight of the woman's ring – a thin band, more precious in sentiment than value. Setting the lantern down and carefully looking around her, she tried to ease it off, but could not shift it beyond the swollen knuckle.

'Come off, come off,' she whispered to herself, her toothless face ghastly in the light of the lantern. 'Fat fingers!' she spat, unaware of Jack Hogg approaching stealthily from the alleyway. He crept up beside her.

'Ah!'

'Murder, ho! Watch!' she screamed.

'Don't ye call for the watch, woman,' rasped Jack.

'Jack Hogg! Thou devil.'

'What ails ye, Doll – fat fingers?'

'I didn't hear ye coming. Where be the bell?'

'With Alf, up the alley. What's afoot, Doll? – A fat finger! What's it attached to?' He shone a lamp into the dead woman's face. 'Ah, 'tis Martha – at last. She did cling on too long – Aha, the ring.'

'Ah, but 'tis only a trifle – not worth much,' said Doll.

'No, no, no – 'tis a nice bit of gold, Doll.'

'Ye have no mercy, Jack Hogg. I did clean and breathe the vapours for a trinket.'

Jack laughed. 'I'll help ye take it off, Doll.'

'Ay, help me take it off. I'll give ye half when I do sell it.'

'Nay, 'tis a fool's job. Get thee gone and bide thy time.'

'Give me the ring!'

'Nay, 'tis mine. Get in,' he said, pushing her towards the house. 'There's a stink to be cleared.'

Doll spat bitterly back: 'The devil Plague take ye!'

After Doll had gone, wildly protesting into Martha's house, there came the loud clanging of a bell.

'Bring out your dead, bring out your dead...'

'Too late – they're brought,' said Jack.

'Oh, 'tis Martha,' said Alf. 'What's she got?'

'A ring,' said Jack.

'Ye have trinkets enough, Jack. Ye can't take it with ye when ye go.'

'Nay,' said Jack, 'but I can try, Alf, I can try.'

20

There was a curfew at this time – not only to prevent the citizens from spreading the plague, but because looting was rife now that shops and warehouses had been deserted. The shopkeepers and merchants who owned them had left the city or been carried off by the plague. Beneficiaries of the dozens of empty premises, which were replete with goods, would not dare to venture into London to claim their inheritances – large or small, during the plague. But if they didn't claim them now, the likes of Jack Hogg would. Business was thriving for him in thievery – now that the constables and watchmen were in short supply. He was suspected of many a theft, though true to the wily nature of his ungodly work he was never caught. To date: he had broken into a warehouse and made off with some bales of wool, into the chandler's shop and stolen candles, and into the wig-maker's, from which he had exited with a bundle of periwigs, though he would find few heads to sell them to now. Wigs were quickly going out of fashion, due to the hair that fashioned them being harvested from the locks of plague victims. But Jack Hogg lived for the day and hadn't thought of that. His hiding place of choice for his booty was the hayloft in the inn-yard.

While Jack was in the hayloft taking stock, a poor old man found a place to sit in the street under the jutting roof of the inn. He was not afflicted by plague, yet begged, for he was insensible in grief and didn't know where to appeal for alms. Yet, even as he told the saddest tale, people ignored his plight. Compassion was in short supply now, as nearly everyone in London had a tragic story to tell and feared catching the plague.

'Ah, 'tis little I did have in the world – scarce but a penny wheaten loaf. Yet I did have a wife, noble as wife can be, and two sons – one to be 'prentice to a wheelwright erelong, my other – a goodly, hard-working lad that did shame me to the core. Now I know not, I know not…'

One or two citizens hurried by, indifferent to his plight. Indifference dealt its own kind of evil, for they passed by caring nothing for him. He watched them, desolate, rambling and scarcely knowing what he spoke.

'I did see them – I did see my dear family tipped into their grave,' he continued mournfully. 'Nay, 'twas not their grave, 'twas shared with dozens more! Their lowly grave was shared with dozens more and I could not lay a flower. I am yet numb with grief. Please…'

Another citizen walked by and said scathingly: 'Shut up old man, for 'tis the same for us all, I tell thee, 'tis the same for us all…'

A rough word in grief in a state of poverty is dreadful to endure, and as though in pity for the lone man crouching there, the sun came from a cloud to warm him. He smiled and said: 'Ah, the sun – 'tis well. I'll lie me down to rest, and I shall die erewhile.'

But the ill-world that London had become morphed into Jack Hogg and begrudged him even that: 'Get up and get out o' the way,' growled Jack, coming from the inn-yard, 'lest I take ye for a corps and bury ye betimes.'

'Nay,' said the poor soul. 'Here is my space – I prithee,

let me stay.'

'Nah, get up and be gone! Get out, I say!' continued Jack, pulling the poor soul to his feet. He had endured enough inconvenience and wanted to get on with his job, for more lucrative jobs awaited him.

It happened that Jack was doing his fellow-citizen a favour, for these were dangerous times. Someone on the edge of death, or perhaps in drunken stupor, may have been bundled up, flung into the cart by mistake and trundled off to the pit-side beneath a pile of bodies. And to be met with this ill-chance was to risk the horror of being buried alive. There was a story going about then: an unwary inebriate was saved from this dreadful fate in the nick of time, because the dead-carter heard him play his cheery pipe. Jack pressed the point.

'Do ye hear?' he bellowed, 'Do ye want to be buried alive?'

It was then that a young woman wearing cloak and hood approached, and said: 'Do ye not recognise the saddler's man? He is a goodly soul, and I would take him with me to give him alms.'

'Ay, take him,' snarled Jack – 'lest he gets scooped up by the dead-cart.'

'The young woman resolved to take the old man to her house and, no sooner had they turned the corner away from the market square, than James called into the victuallers nearby. He didn't notice the significance of the young woman and the old man turning into the square on route to Church Lane.

When they arrived at her home, the maid brought some wheaten bread and broth and a tankard of warm ale for the old man. He ate and drank hungrily and, after a welcome repast, began to gather his senses.

'I did think it was an angel I did see before me by the inn,' he said. 'I would surely have died a nobody, yet ye made me feel a worthy man.'

'I have seen ye at thy work in the saddler shop,' she said. 'Indeed, ye are a worthy man. Thy name is Thomas, is it not?'

'Ay, but I no longer have work, for the saddler did turn me out when my family fell sick, but God spared me. I know not why. Why did God spare me and take my wife and sons before me? Why did I deserve such good fortune where there is none?'

'It is not a question I can answer but I can tell thee that I do not need a saddler, but that my gardener hath gone and I do need another. I have a large brick shed – 'tis almost a small house, if ye would care to share it with the plants. There is salt-fish, cheese, and broth and wheaten bread – 'tis simple, but 'tis goodly fare.'

'Madam, I do thank thee from my heart, and would be pleased to work in thy garden – yet still I do wonder at my good fortune when...'

A lump in his throat prevented another utterance and the lady took his hand. So many grieving souls wanted an answer. 'Why did I survive and my family perish?'

It remained a mystery. The greatest fatalities arose among those who lived close together or gathered in groups. Yet there were exceptions. Some, who were locked away for forty days in a household ripe with plague, prevailed and walked out of the house alive, while others, lonely and sequestered, succumbed to the disease and were taken. The reason that the plague struck in such a random way was a question that even the physicians couldn't answer.

'Ye ask why ye deserved such good fortune – why ye should be spared and thy family taken. I cannot answer that,' said the lady, 'for no one yet knows the reason. But for myself, my good fortune would be in Heaven. Let that thought be of comfort to thee.'

'Ye would rather die?'

'If it is written.'

'I have seen thee in the church, praying alone. What is thy name?'

'My name, Thomas? It is Jessica.'

21

Later that evening, James ventured to the riverside alone. He knew that this was a dangerous place, for it was close to the abandoned warehouses targeted by robbers. Moreover, there was scarcely a constable to keep the looters away. But hearing that the afflicted were accustomed to run out of their houses and jump into the Thames distracted, he felt obliged to reason with them and save their souls. He had been afraid, and it came as a relief to him when he arrived to find everything still and quiet, without any souls to save, and he enjoyed a moment's peace as he stood by the quayside.

Along the Thames he could see ferries, lighters and other vessels bobbing at their moorings. Their lanterns blinked, reflecting light into the ripples below. People were living in those boats James had been told, closed up, isolated from the land, sitting it out until the vapours passed. It was said that a good living could be had for anyone willing to row out to supply victuals.

James was just wondering about the people who were preserving their lives in this way, when he heard a noise coming from a warehouse behind him and, with unaccustomed bravado, he approached.

'What noise? What noise, I say?'

As he challenged them, two girls danced carelessly past, chattering and giggling – each wearing a high-crowned hat with a nodding feather and playing with fripperies.

'Ay, 'tis a pretty riband,' laughed one.

'Mine is prettier,' said the other – 'but I do not like the hat.'

'Nay, 'tis high-crowned.'

'Ay, 'tis not of the fashion, but it doth become a wench!'

James hurried towards them and motioned them to stop, but they continued to laugh loudly and caper about like fools.

'In God's name, what mischief is this? Do ye not know that the curfew bell hath rung that the sick might take the air?'

Again, they danced – now slowly – as though in a sick parody of the times.

'We do be sad and merry, and we do take the air,' said one – more impertinent than the other. 'Do ye like my riband, sir? Shall I tie my hair?'

'Merciful God, what have ye done?'

The impertinent one made no excuses for their conduct. 'Done? Do ye not see? – Hats and ribands – 'tis hats and ribands,' she said with a twirl.

'What is this thievery?' asked James, and she laughed the more.

By now, James was red in the face with anger: 'Answer me, I say, for 'tis shame on thee!' He moved to apprehend them but stopped suddenly as young lady wearing a hooded cloak appeared breathlessly from around the corner.

'Peg!' she called, anxiously. 'What have ye done?'

'Madam!' cried the girl.

Jessica removed her hood.

'Jessica!'

'James!'

'What do ye here?' he asked.

'Peg – return what ye have taken to the warehouse and go ye home. Audrey must return to her house and not call on thee again. By and by, I shall speak to thee.'

'Ay, madam,' and they walked solemnly away.

'What means this, Jessica? What do ye here?' asked James, bewildered.

'I followed my maid, for she had been drinking mead with her friend – the tanner's girl. They were merry, sir, for I suspect that they did think the mead would prevent the plague. I saw the cellar open and the empty bottle down upon the ground and did hurry hither after them.'

'But why did they behave thus?'

'I do not know. Perchance they do play their last, for they believe tomorrow may be their last, and they knew not what to do. Peg was nearly sent to the pest-house when we prepared to leave for Huntingdon, for we could not take her with us. I did speak for her, that she might stay and keep the house in order, but she is young and too often grows afraid. She did fret and say the hooves of death would stop outside our door. She was distracted – 'tis why they drank the mead, and...'

'Nay, Jessica. I ask why are ye here? Lady – to see ye here among these ever- growing woes is both shock and gladness. I bethought me ye did go forth to Huntingdon. Wherefore do I find ye still?'

They sat down on the barrels by the stair that led down to the quay.

'For that I was abandoned, sir,' she said.

'Abandoned? What mean ye?'

'I do think – 'twas fate's plan.'

'Nay, I do not believe in augers.'

'Yet let me tell thee. An hour before the time to leave I did sneeze.'

'Bless us, no!'

'Ne'er was there such a sneeze. I was shocked and fearful – for a moment frozen in eternity – ere my poor parents knew what they would do or say. My mother wailed and wept enough to start the heavens, and my father did strut about the room in ill-kept circles, whereupon I cried out in despair that I should stay. It was a sad parting.'

'Sad, indeed.'

'For three days I did wait. For three days, I prayed. Young Peg did nurse me day and night, glad of the company – and I was saved.'

'Thanks be to God!'

'Ay, for that it was a common cold, and we did think that I had caught the plague.'

'I have heard such tales before. Oh, Jessica, I am truly glad to see thee well. So too am I glad that ye do remain among us here to lighten the darkness – though it is unworthy of me to say so.'

She looked up at him. 'Nay, 'tis not unworthy, James – for I am glad I did not go.'

He would have kissed her then. 'Jessica, I must take thee to thy house, for truly, 'tis not the time for us to talk like this. When the evil plague is gone...'

'When the evil plague is gone, what then, James?'

'What ho! Who stirs? Do ye be sick or well?' demanded the watchman.

'Well, and 'tis only I, the priest. I do but comfort souls,' answered James.

'Ah – best go indoors, 'tis a dangerous time...'

Suddenly, a family of five, living opposite the warehouse, climbed from the top window and clambered over the roof, slipping and sliding and calling to one another for help...

'What was that?' asked the watch, shifting himself. 'Now there's the cheek. They do climb from the window – Hey! You there! They do escape, for I have turned my back. Hey, stop! In the name of the Lord Mayor – of the King – stop! Constable, they do escape!' The watchman hurried off looking for the constable but there was no constable to come.

'God speed!' waved Jessica. 'To Lock the healthy away with the sick is wickedness, and 'tis good the poor people do think up ways to confound the watch.'

'Ay, 'tis much easier to escape now,' said James, 'for the plague doth progress and take the law with it. There is only one to guard a house now, and little order. I have heard they do go into the night to take their chances in the fields.'

'Then God go with them,' said Jessica.

'Amen.' As he rose to help her up, a passing dead-cart sprayed mud at them.

'Oh! My dress!' cried Jessica.'

'And on thy face. Take my kerchief, 'tis fresh from the laundry woman this morn.'

Jessica quickly mopped her face and lamented the state of her dress. 'On the morrow I must wear something meet.'

'Ye shall not walk abroad on the morrow,' he said

'Oh, but I shall.'

'Nay, tis unwise…'

'I shall be judge of that,' she asserted.

'I shall take charge of thee for thy parents, for ye are not of age.'

'My father durst not rule me, nor shall ye.'

He knew that he stood on a powder keg. 'We will argue no longer. I shall take thee home lest another disaster befall thee. The watch speaks true.'

They walked in silence. It was a dismal scene on the way through to Church Lane. The sick ranged about the streets with nowhere to turn for relief. Two sat entwined beneath the water pump in the square, clutching each other in the vague hope of comfort – each of them displaying their rashes, sores, and great boils that throbbed with pain. Sometimes the priest averted his eyes at the chilling sights before him, but Jessica looked on in disbelief as they passed.

'See how they suffer,' she said, as they walked beneath the archway into the square. 'It should not be possible to imagine how they feel – and yet I can, for 'tis as though I wear their shoes.'

'I would not have thee wear their shoes,' laughed James.

'Do not laugh! I do mean – 'tis a little more than sympathy, yet cannot be empathy. I do wonder – nay, have decided, 'tis of moment. Ye will say 'tis a foolish thought…'

'What foolish thought is this?'

'That I would nurse the sick.'

'The plague-struck?'

'Ay.'

'Nay, lady – truly 'tis a foolish thought – to work among the filthy streets and breathe the wicked vapours. So far ye are preserved. For that ye must thank God.'

'Which God is that? The God that bids me turn away? The God that strikes us down for naught?'

He didn't answer her, but the barb struck home, and they said no more as they walked along the lane until they reached her gate.

'Shut ye indoors, Jessica, and never from your casement once look out – until the plague be spent.'

'Oh, no, I cannot stay within,' she said.

'Cannot?'

'Shall not.'

'How so?'

'I did already tell thee. I shall help the sick.'

'Nay, Jessica – and catch the plague?'

'The doctor hath not caught it.'

'The doctor drinks too much. I would not have thee a drunkard!'

She laughed. 'Ye are not a drunkard, and yet have not caught the plague.'

'The good Lord hath preserved me.'

'So too shall the good Lord preserve me. Oh, I have seen such sights tonight that seared my heart.'

'There is nothing ye can do, Jessica,' he said.

'Ay, there is something, for I shall not abide their suffering. Ye are not my keeper, James.'

'Nay – I tell thee this: the good doctor shall not let ye

work among the filthy streets to tend the plague. E'en now ye have mud on thy shoes and their delicate bows, and all about the hem of thy skirt.'

'I have shoes and skirts meet for the filthy streets, and have no need of bows.'

'Ye are a lady…'

'I'll none of this. Goodnight, sir.'

'Goodnight – and mark me. Ye have mud on thy nose.'

22

The following evening, the doctor was in his cups and had gone to sleep. He was asleep for little more than an hour when there was a knock at the door. 'Is there no rest?' he wailed, for he had been working for more than a day, with no respite, and cursed the name of Doctor. There came another knock. 'Ay, ay, I am coming! – I need the patience of a saint.' He had no housekeeper left to respond to callers, and his maid had gone home, so he opened up the door himself. He was amazed to see Jessica there so late.

'I must see the doctor,' she said, in an imperious tone. She did not recognise him, for he had left his periwig hanging on a nail. He stood alarmed, his bald head shining in the light of the lamp.

'It is I,' he said.

'What is this trick? I demand to see the doctor,' and with a flounce of her skirt, she passed him by and entered his study when, beholding his empty chair and his periwig hanging on a nail, exclaimed: 'Oh, Lord!'

The doctor grabbed his wig, as though his life depended on it, and slipped it on his naked head without arrangement. 'What mean thee, Jessica, to come upon me at this hour? – Oh, I pray 'tis not the vapours. Are ye sick?'

'Nay. I am yet well, and I do repent me. To come upon thee at this hour was too unkind. Yet I did mean well.'

'Meant ye well? I tried to rest, for I have not slept for more than four and twenty hours...'

'That I do know, doctor, and that – in part – is why I come,' she said, offering him a basket of freshly cut herbs. 'I bring some physic from my herb garden that I know will be of use, and some pomanders I did make from aromatic lavender...'

'These are welcome dear lady, and I am grateful to ye, but they could have waited till the morrow. What do ye in London Town?'

She explained in brief.

The doctor nodded: 'It doth happen. Yet why venture out so late among the filthy streets, for who knows who may walk abroad?'

'For that I cannot not rest at night. My brain teems with so many sights of woe – I cannot endure it – unless – I needs must be of use, to nurse the sick and help thee in thy work...'

'Ye, Jessica? For that, I am grateful, but...'

'Ye are exhausted, and it is for this that – the true reason – I am here. So too for the sick who know not where to turn for love and sustenance.' She spread out her hands before him. 'These hands that idled are unused to work, but work they must, to minister to the sick.'

The doctor turned to look at her, and her eyes shone back in earnest. 'There are few goodly nurse-keepers left, and those that do remain are harsh and cruel. I have heard ungodly things about the streets. That is why I offer thee my help, and in turn do offer it to the sick.'

'I do thank thee for thy herbs and for thy pains but must refuse thy goodly offer, Jessica.'

'Why so?'

'For that this is too horrible to contemplate – a lady such as ye in conditions such as these?'

'But, doctor, I entreat thee...'

There came another knock at the door. 'I shall have no legs left,' muttered the doctor. He hurried to open it, to discern his friend standing in the half-light. 'James! What mean ye here?'

'For that I was worried, doctor. Ye have seemed ill of late, and prompted by my prayers I did come hither.'

'I do thank thee,' said the doctor, growing agitated. 'I am not ill – but must have rest, and pity 'tis that friends do bother me.'

'I beg thy pardon, dear friend – I yet meant well...'

'Well? – Ye all mean well. God let me rest!'

'Ay. God rest ye, my friend. I shall see thee on the morrow.'

'Nay, stay ye a while. The lady Jessica is within.'

'Jessica? She is within?' His heart began to pound. 'What brings her here so late? Her name and mischief are conjoined.'

The doctor chuckled. 'Come in and hear our conference,' he said, and he led the way with his candle: 'The priest comes hither, Jessica,' he said.

'Good even, lady,' said James. 'I am amazed to find thee here so late.'

'And I, thee. What doth the priest here so late in the even – when he should be tucked up in bed with his toys?' she teased.

James shook his head. 'I do not laugh,' he said.

'To the matter,' said the doctor, lighting another candle. 'Jessica doth want to help me nurse the sick,

James. What think ye to that?'

'Nay, Jessica – again I say 'tis no work for a lady such as thee,' said James.

'What is a lady such as I? Must she sit and sew and sing and play the lute?'

'If she so desires.'

'Can she not be of use?'

'A lady is not made to be of use in such a way.'

'How not in such a way? I am amazed, sir, that ye should think so lightly of a lady.'

'I do not think lightly of thee, Jessica, but would not have thee catch the plague.'

'All London is a cesspool – I would catch the plague where're I be. I would rather die of use – than sit at home waiting for death to whip me to the grave.'

'Death will not enter in thy home, I shall forbid it,' said James softly.

'My maid tells me that it hath already come to the house. She hath a haunted look upon her face and daily she runs mad.'

'Then send her to the pest-house. She will be well provided for.'

'I shall not! She would run madder still! I do not treat my servants thus.' Earnestly she put her case. 'So many people suffer, sir, and there is no tender hand to mop their brows, to give a sip of ale, to clean the...'

'Desist!' he cut in, grimacing. 'Such filthy work is not for thee to do.'

'Then who will do it? There are none gentle.'

'Then let there be none, and go ye home,' he told her, but as she argued with him, defiant, he knew that she was capable of the task – remembering the draper's girl – and would have told her so, had he not been so fearful for her life. 'Send thy maid to fetch provisions,' he said at last. 'Do not let me see thee wander abroad again – until the plague be spent.'

She laughed. 'Suddenly bold! He who blushed and dithered in my presence doth now lay down the law.' But in serious tone, she turned again to the doctor. 'Doctor, I bid thee change thy mind. I know I am a goodly nurse.'

'Nay, I cannot, Jessica. Go thy ways, dear soul,' and with an exhausted wave of the hand, said: 'James, I beg thee, take the lady home.'

'I shall be glad to see her safely to her house,' said James.

'Ay, 'tis good,' returned the doctor, 'for the hour is late and the way dangerous.' He reached for a lantern and lit it. 'Take a lantern, for there are few lamps hereabouts.'

The doctor was right. For the vulnerable, to walk alone – day or night – was perilous. It was becoming dark now, and God knows what horrors may be lurking within the stench about the streets and alleyways and down the lane to her home, for death had stalked and done its worst, too often leaving poor souls stranded at random around corners, on steps – clinging to their last breath or expiring it.

Thieves roamed the city, ready to strip the dead and dying of the poor few clothes and trinkets they had. Even a winding sheet was worth a penny or two to be sold to the next victim, and stolen from the same victim, when the time was ripe, to sell again. The doctor and James imagined well that Jessica, dressed in her best silks and adornments, would have attracted every rogue within a mile – not forgetting that Jack Hogg roamed at large. This evening, unseen, he had followed her from the shadows to the doctor's, and was still lurking under the archway, as though in sleep with his hat pulled down over his face, hoping that she would soon return home alone in the dark.

'Sir John hath told me that there are few constables to keep the thieves away, and no longer can the streets be cleared at night ready for the next day, for he doth lack the rakers – and those who would clear away the bodies that pile up faster than they can be thrown into the carts,' said the doctor, with a last spurt of energy.

'Ay, 'tis a scene from Hell itself,' said James. 'I never thought that London Town would come to such a pass.' He turned to Jessica. 'I know ye will not obey me, lady – for again I see that I am out of favour – yet I trust that ye will heed the doctor.'

'For the good doctor's sake, I shall go with thee,' she conceded and, raising her kerchief to her face, she left the house. James followed after her, leaving the doctor nodding in his chair.

They stepped into the silent street. 'Take my arm,' said James, but she declined and continued to walk ahead.

'Forgive me if I do not speak to thee,' she turned and said, 'for I no longer have a thing to say.'

'Then God is merciful to me,' said James, and as she turned into the alley, he heard a stifled scream and hastened after her. Holding the lantern aloft, he shone it upon Jack Hogg.

'Jack Hogg, thou devil!' he exclaimed, for the wretch had Jessica pinned to the wall.

Jack looked up suddenly, his fiendish face lit one side by the lantern. 'The priest — in hell where he belongs!' and thrusting Jessica aside, he drew back his fist and made to knock him flat. As he did so, James swung the lantern, glancing a heavy blow on Jack's brow and, muttering filthy oaths, the wretch made off into the darkness.

'Ye reaped what ye did sow, Jessica,' said James, taking her by the hand. 'I trust ye shall no longer seek to walk abroad on such a night.'

She sulked and didn't speak to him until they reached Church Lane when, unclasping her hand and remaining petulant, she said. 'I could have sown much good, 'twere not for thee, for ye did not help my cause.'

'I think ye know, I did,' he said, 'or ye would be in the alley now — a victim of Jack Hogg.'

He saw, by the lantern, a tear glint in her eye. 'I did want to nurse the poor sick souls that have no-one to help them.'

'Lady,' he said, setting the lantern down on the wall by her gate, 'I ask thee, think no more of this. I prithee, stay inside.'

She said nothing for a while, as though carefully choosing her words, then said quickly: 'I do repent me if I caused ye danger in the alley, but...'

'I thank thee for thy penitence.'

'Yet it doth not mean I can be told by thee.'

He laughed. 'I tell thee a thousand times I do know that lady.'

'Ah, 'tis as it should be. Why do ye look at me thus?'

'Because the moon came from a cloud and shone upon thy face.'

'So too it shone on thine. What means this tender look?'

'That I would kiss thee if I dared.' He could not believe the boldness of his words.

'Then I dare thee to.'

'Nay – for I do fear...'

'The plague? They say an ill-star reign. If 'tis true, and die we must, shall we not die kissed?'

'Then shall I challenge death.'

He leaned forward to kiss her, but she turned away and, stepping back, he propelled himself into the rose bush. He emerged in a tangle of thorns. 'The devil!'

He didn't see her smile beneath her kerchief.

'Ye have challenged me. Wherefore should we kiss, for half an hour hence ye did rule me. My father durst not do it, or my mother. I rule myself!'

'Jessica!'

'I do as I please and thou shalt know it!'

He paused for dignity: 'Lady, there is a plague abroad. Each time ye do walk out of thy door, death lies in wait. I do not try to rule thee but to preserve thee.'

'I have looked death in the face and it hath turned away, for 'tis fear itself that should be feared.'

She left him with no words of combat. In stunned silence he walked away – just as the moon slunk under a cloud.

23

The following day, Jessica paced about the house. She had been misunderstood. She had offered herself to the service of the sick – daring the plague – yet had been rejected. What good could she do now, parading a silk dress and fluttering a fan when all around London Town people were dying in distress? She knew that the sick craved gentleness and compassion in the last moments of their lives.

Yesterday, a woman sobbing in an alley had reached out to her in pleading. Kneeling down beside her, Jessica held the woman's hand and said: 'Do not be afraid that it grows dark, for the other side of the door is light.' The woman died contented. At that moment the constable walked by: 'Go thee home lady or ye will ruin thy pretty dress,' he said. Remembering his words, she realised that it was her dress that was a bar to her.

Thinking this, she stopped pacing about and placed one hand upon her brow, the other against her stomacher. Suddenly it struck her. The constable would not have moved her on, or the doctor reject her help, if she had been dressed in linen. Her privilege was a disadvantage to her, and she made up her mind to return to the doctor – in disguise.

The plague had a strange effect on Peg. Earlier she was in a screaming fit. Now she sat sedately in the house-keeper's room, mending her skirts and singing folk songs. Singing lifted her spirits, she said, and kept the Reaper away. She looked up from her sewing when Jessica came in.

'Are ye better now, Peg?'

'Ay, madam. I am mending my skirts, for they are old.'

'Ye need new ones, but 'tis difficult to buy linen now, for the merchants have gone and the shops are closed up. When the plague is over, we shall to the tailor and ye shall have new clothes.' She looked from the window to see the old man in the garden. 'How fares our poor guest?'

'I did as ye asked, madam. I gave him more broth – and he sleeps in the shed. He did say he would help me in the garden on the morrow.'

'He does well. – Oh, this corset. It pinches. Unlace it, Peg.'

'Ay, madam. I wonder what it would be like to dress like a lady,' she said, loosening the laces.

'It looks pretty, but 'tis uncomfortable,' said Jessica.

'Ye may have this old thing, instead – 'tis comfortable, madam,' said Peg, who secretly envied her mistress's fine clothes.

Jessica contemplated.

Yes, that was the answer! She would return to the doctor's in the disguise of a humble nurse-keeper.

'The streets are so dirty. I think I should wear something simpler and easy to clean…Calm ye, Peg. What ails ye?'

'Naught, madam.'

The maid changed with the moment. Again, she was fearful of the plague.

'There is something,' persisted Jessica, 'Pray God ye are not ill.'

'Ill? Oh, the dear Lord!' She cringed in the corner,

rocking backwards and forwards as though mad.

Jessica knew the signs – the defensive body language, the fear in the maid's eyes. 'Ye may go now,' she said. 'Drink some hot milk and garlic and rest.'

'Ay, madam.'

'But before ye go, where do ye keep thy old clothes?'

'In the big linen chest on the landing, madam – and some that I wore as the kitchen maid.'

'Thank ye, Peg. I would borrow them. Go ye now – and try to sleep.'

With a parting bob, the maid, now recovered from her moment's madness, went to her room, leaving Jessica to explore the contents of the heavy trunk. The humble clothes fitted perfectly, and were so much more practical. She pulled the linen cap over her curls. The simple dress was harsh upon her skin, for she was used to silk, but it had to be endured. The freshly-laundered apron looked too clean to be believed. If she was to be accepted as a nurse-keeper, she must dirty it – not too much – and for another authentic touch, she pricked her finger on a pin to smear a spot of blood amongst the dirt. Newly dressed as a nurse-keeper, she looked in the heavy mirror in the hall, but still saw Jessica looking back at her. The dark hair that fringed the cap was hers, so too was the face – and she must not be discovered until the plague had done its worst.

Now, she went downstairs into the kitchen with a plan. It was not her domain and she looked about her in wonder. The gleaming brass pots and copper pans, the heavy iron cauldron hanging on a hook in the hearth, the giant meat plates in a rack, dishes and collection of knives and cooking implements, all fascinated her, but there was nothing of use to the purpose. She opened another door leading from the kitchen where she beheld a wash tub and a scrubbing board, and in the corner a large mangle with a washing basket by its side. Back in the kitchen, she tried another door that opened into the larder. There were sundry vegetables in baskets on the floor and, on the shelf, a meat safe with nothing in it, a large jar of salted fish, another of dried peas, half a wheaten loaf – protected from the mice – a covered butter dish and one of cheese, a jug of milk…Jessica ran her finger along the heavy jars until she found one labelled: 'Flour'. At last she found what she was looking for. She rubbed some flour into her surrounding hair to tone it down and went upstairs from the kitchen and out into the kitchen garden. Taking some dirt, she rubbed it across her face and went to her room.

Jessica looked in the mirror again, and no longer saw herself looking back at her, but a humble nurse-keeper. Her disguise was complete and, coming upon Peg, who had now usurped the house-keeper's room, frightened the maid out of her wits.

'Help! Madam! Come quickly, 'tis a ruffian come to burgle!' she squealed.

'Calm ye down,' said Jessica and, removing the cap, said: 'See, 'tis I, and ye did not recognise me.'

'Nay, madam – 'tis truly a disguise.'

'I have a secret, Peg,' said Jessica. She had no choice but to tell the girl, and begged her confidence.

'Nay, 'tis dangerous, madam…'

'That I do know, but I would nurse the sick and there

is no other way.'

'Ay, madam.'

'Keep close indoors or in the garden for the produce. There are potatoes, turnips and cabbages ripe for harvest. The gardener shall understand my plan.'

'Ay, madam. He works uncommon hard. He digs the ground and pulls out the weeds, madam – but does worry about the roses. He says that when they open, they do die.'

'Ay, 'tis strange,' she said. 'And Peg – If someone should come by and ask for me, tell them I do not wish to go abroad but yet am well.'

'I shall, madam.'

'Ye are a trusty maid, Peg.'

'When go ye, madam – to the sick?'

'I go first to the doctor's house this eventide. Feed thy selves well, and make broth for Thomas. Remember that ye are safe within the house. Ye do not need to holler. Do not venture abroad – unless to buy a wheaten loaf – and that before noon. The mayor doth still ensure a good supply.'

'Ay, madam.'

'Do not tarry in the town.'

'Oh, no, I would not.'

As dusk fell, Jessica left the house through the back gate and, carefully looking around her, saw a fox slinking in the lane: 'Shoo! Shoo!' she whispered, 'They will kill thee, else.' The fox ran off and, in the guise of a humble nurse-keeper, she stepped towards the doctor's house. The way was not as clear as it had been the night before, and she was unprepared for the grisly sights she saw in the streets and alleys on the way. For the cart had not yet come to claim them, and the bodies of poor souls departed in every aspect of pain and terror, lay strewn along the way.

24

The doctor was not at home when Jessica arrived. She was informed by a surly maid that he'd gone to a meeting at the College of Physicians, and told to wait in his study. 'Sit there and don't ye steal trinkets,' said the maid. Although other than books, a goose-quill pen and sundry glass containers with goodness-know-what floating about in them, there were no trinkets to be had.

Jessica was shocked. Was this what it felt like to wear these lowly clothes – to be spoken down to and insulted? 'Ye must not speak to me thus,' she said.

The housemaid looked her up and down, suspiciously. 'I'll speak to ye how I want. What d' ye do – to talk like a duchess in a 'guise?'

At once, she realised her mistake. What was the good of her disguise if she spoke in her usual manner? She thought about it quickly. 'Ye did think I was someone!' she laughed. 'I do like to play the fool!'

Suddenly, a cry from a child could be heard nearby, and the housemaid tutted and left the room.

Jessica thought it was as well that she had been taken unawares before the doctor arrived, for he would have recognised her for certain by her manner of speech. Some minutes later, she heard voices just outside the door. It was the doctor with James! Her heart thumped. She looked behind her, but the window was high and she had no means of escape. As they entered, she stood up, head bowed, and feigned subservience.

'What means this mistress?' asked the doctor.

'I was turned out of doors and do look for work, sir,'

she said – in a quiet, diffident, unfamiliar manner. She dared not look at James in the course of the conversation.

'Sit ye down, James,' said the doctor, nodding towards the chair in the corner. 'What kind of work do ye seek, girl? As ye see, I have a housemaid. Can ye cook?'

Her heart sank as she searched for an answer. 'Nay,' she said at last, adopting a breathy tone of voice, 'my broth doth not taste well sir, I burn the pastry when I do make it, and my buns are like stones, sir. I did get sent out of the kitchen.'

'This speaks of disaster – doth it not, James?'

'The devil's feast,' doctor.

'I am disappointed, for I do need a cook,' the good doctor said.

'They did say ye wanted another nurse, sir,' she said tentatively. 'I can dress wounds. I did dress wounds in a house, but all the family hath been taken, sir.'

'Ay, 'tis true – but 'tis filthy work for one so young as ye. Ay, 'tis certain I could use ye as a nurse-keeper, for there are many sick to care for – two in my house, all about the parish, in the pest-house... Nay, 'tis filthy work to clean the blood and pus and...'

'I do know about it. See my apron, sir.'

The doctor looked at her kindly and said: 'Nay – ye are too young. I would not have ye carried off with the vapours. I shall speak to the Lord Mayor, for he may need a goodly servant.'

'I have breathed the vapours all the while – but I chew garlic all the while, sir.'

'Do ye? Well, 'tis uncommon, sweet breath that doth chew garlic all the while,' said the doctor.

'Ah – There was none in the market, sir, all the week,' she said quickly.

'Yet still ye remain well?'

The doctor was aware of certain citizens who went among the sick, yet – as though charmed – never caught the infection. He knew a physician in a nearby parish who, not only dressed wounds, let blood and applied leeches, but was inquisitive enough to bend over his distempered victims in order to smell their stinking breath! Yet he was the healthiest of physicians. All this he contemplated. He turned to James: 'What think ye, James?'

James shook his head, and said impatiently: 'Doctor, 'tis not my decision, tis thine. I do but come to get the plague water ye promised. I must no longer stay – for I have business at the church – I dare not think of the madness by the pit.'

'Ay, James, I do apologise. I did forget.' He reached up to the shelf and brought down a bottle and handing it to James said, 'See, 'tis writ on the bottle how to take.'

'I do thank thee, doctor.' Going towards the door, James turned and added: 'For the girl – if ye ask – she seems a goodly soul, and ye do need the help. Ye could do worse. Fare thee well.'

'Fare thee well, James.'

Jessica watched him leave the room, prayer book in his hand. Then, breathing a lengthy sigh, she turned again to the doctor: 'Well, sir?'

'I do warn thee, 'tis a cesspit.'

133

'Ay, that I do know,' she said. 'But I must work. I shall starve, else.'

'What is thy name?'

There was an uneasy pause. She hadn't thought of that.

'Ye do not know thy name?' he probed.

'My real name?' she said at length.

'Ay.'

'Oh,' she said at last, 'my real name is Margaret, but they do call me Meg.'

'Then 'tis Meg.'

There came another cry from the next room and the doctor shook his head. 'I can no longer parley, for I have remedies to mix.   Go ye to the room next door – the boy doth cry in pain. Do what ye can to stop his holler until I come to attend to him.'

'I thank ye, sir. I shall be good help to thee.'

'Ha, 'tis well the proof will not be in the pudding!'

'For sure I am a better nurse than cook, sir.'

'I am thankful for that.'

'Where shall I go?' she asked, acting a little foolish.

'Go to the room next door where the poor boy hollers. Go to, go to,' he said, with a peremptory wave of the hand.

A boy of about seven years old lay on a truckle bed covered with a thick blanket. His cry had been reduced to a sob and stopped when Jessica came into the room.

'Good even, boy,' she said, and the boy hid down the bed.

'Oh!' she exclaimed, pulling the blanket away, 'this blanket is too hot and coarse. Ye shall have a clean sheet of linen – after I have washed thy dirty face and hands.' She went to the water pump and returned with a bowl of cold water, a flannel and a towel.

He looked up at her warily, the dirt on his face mingled with tears. Jessica placed her hand on his brow and her face lit up. 'God be praised, ye have no fever!'

'No fever?'

'It means ye are well.'

'They do not come to take me?'

'Take thee where, little boy?'

'To that place.'

She sat down beside him and, while she washed his hands and face, encouraged him to talk: 'What place is that?'

'Where the cart doth go,' and he hid himself under the sheet.

'Tell me where the cart goes and why it is taking thee,' she said, 'Did ye have a bad dream?'

'Nay.' Responding to her gentleness he emerged from under the sheet, his eyes wide with terror. 'It came at night,' he said, 'and they did take my mother, my father, my sister and my uncle, and did shout and ring a bell, and they did throw my family into the cart and take them away to the pit. They did take them to the pit!' And he wept again.

Jessica wiped away his tears and listened patiently as he told a fragmented story from the beginning and, little by little, she pieced it together.

It was three weeks ago that his father, a tailor, was taken ill with sickness and fever. The examiner of health arrived soon afterwards and reported their house infected, and notice was given for it to be locked up for forty days – with the whole family inside. Two watchmen, bearing halberds, stood either side of the door after it was locked up, lest the family should try to escape. The rest of the family wailed and wept and cried out to be set free from the vapours within, but Jacob stayed in his room much of the time singing happy songs. His mother died, and his sister grieved so much that she died the next day. An old uncle in the house was so shocked at the deaths coming one after the other that he sat silently and shook in terror, and he too died the day afterwards. Jacob sang his songs the whole time, for he said it made him feel better. He began to be afraid only when a woman came to the house with a red stick to search out the dead – prodding and poking at his family. The dead-cart had arrived soon afterwards, and he described the brutal way his family was treated by the collectors of the dead. He couldn't sing happy songs anymore after that. He was sitting in the street outside his house when the doctor found him. The boy was so dirty, and wailing as though in pain, that he was believed to be infected by his family. In an act of kindness, the doctor brought him to this house intent on nursing him – as physicians were often obliged to nurse the sick.

Jessica was moved by his sad story and could have wept for him. 'Oh, bless thee,' she said, 'ye do not weep with pain for ye are well. I know which cart ye mean. Oh, poor, poor boy. But ye are not ill. Oh, thank God for that,' she said, overjoyed for the little soul.

'Nay,' I do not think I am ill. Every day I do wake alive.'

'And ye shall wake alive tomorrow, and the next day

and the next. Ye do not have the plague, and ye shall not go in the cart.'

'I am not going?'

'I shall not let thee. What is thy name?'

'Jacob. What is thine?'

'Jess, just call me nurse. And now that ye have clean face and hands, I shall find thee another shirt to wear.' She found a clean shirt belonging to the doctor. 'We shall borrow it,' she said, and rolled up the sleeves to fit.

When the doctor returned, he was astounded to see that the boy was sitting up on his truckle bed. He was laughing and had a clean face, wore a capacious shirt and had a clean sheet across his knees.

'He doth want some broth,' said Jessica.

'But I did come to treat wounds,' said the doctor.

'Ye shall not need to treat wounds, for he is well. He hath no fever and no signs of the evil plague.' She explained the boy's dilemma. 'He was covered in filth and muck, and cried in terror – not in pain. His name is Jacob.'

'Well, Jacob, I am glad to see thee so well,' said the doctor. 'We did worry that ye were very sick – and now ye are hungry?'

'Ay,' said Jacob, 'for I could eat a horse.'

'Nay, horses are in short supply. Ye cannot eat a horse. What say ye to a bowl of broth and wheaten bread dipped in it?'

'Ay, sir.'

The doctor took Jessica aside and said: 'He shall eat well. I shall bid the housemaid make the broth. On the morrow, ye must take him to the pest-house for there they shall feed him well.'

'But the pest-house be crowded with the sick,' she said in alarm.

'And with the well,' said the doctor. 'Nay, 'twill be good for him, for he is an orphan with no-one to care for him. The parish shall organise alms well.'

'But I do not think…'

'Ye are uncommon bold,' said the doctor. 'On the morrow, early – for there is much work to do – ye shall take him in a Hackney coach to the pest-house. It is for the best, for we cannot keep him here. I shall need the room.'

Jessica knew that the Hackney coaches were filthy, and never would she care to step into one – well aware that they often conveyed, not only the plague victims, but those who didn't realise that they harboured the infection. The idea of riding in one, together the little boy, to deposit him into the pest-house that accommodated sick and well alike, was abhorrent. Yet, there was no doubt that she would have been discovered had she further challenged the doctor, who, to his credit, meant no ill. He was far too inundated with work to notice the state of the Hackney coaches, and again she was obliged to feign subservience.

'Ay, sir, I shall take him on the morrow,' she said.

But nurse-keeper had no intention of doing so.

In the morning, very early, she and Jacob left the doctor's as she had promised, but instead of getting a Hackney coach, holding his hand she stole through the archway into and beyond the market square to Church

Lane. Mercifully, the streets had been cleared of bodies the night before and she could see no sick taking the air so early.

Jacob was anxious. 'Where are we going, nurse?'

'Ye may call me Jessica now,' she said, 'and we are going somewhere that ye can sing all day long if it pleases ye.'

As they came through the gate past the old brick shed, Jessica was amazed to see the garden taking shape again – with weeds and deadwood piled in neat heaps, and some produce harvested and stored in wooden boxes. Suddenly something sprang out of one of the boxes and leapt up through window of the brick shed.

'Look, 'tis a cat!' cried Jacob.

'Nay, there are no cats left in London,' said Jessica.

'Ay!' he cried, 'In there!'

Jessica knew that many of the citizens in London had two or three cats before the plague. The fact that they kept so many was because the cats preyed on the rats and mice that inhabited the squalid environment at the time. Yet in their ill-wisdom, at the advent of the plague, the authorities destroyed the poor cats in their thousands, leaving London Town overrun with rats which harboured the vectors of the plague – fleas. This cat, that had only one eye, had surely escaped the massacre and was probably living courtesy of Thomas the new gardener. Jessica greeted Peg at the door, and gave her the care of little Jacob, before asking the question.

'Hath the gardener a cat, Peg?'

'Nay, madam.'

'I shall ask thee again. Hath the gardener a cat?'

'He might do, madam.'

'He doth, Peg.'

'It was hiding under that fallen tree by the shed madam – 'twas the killers – and the cat has done no harm. And Thomas did give it a name. He doth call it Cyclops, for it only hath one eye. Will ye tell?'

'Nay, Peg. I shall not tell, for I do not believe that the cats carried the plague – 'tis more like rats – I am glad for the cat to stay and kill the rats. There is salt fish and milk?'

'Ay, madam, and there is yet fish in the market and it can eat the skins.'

'Do not feed it too well, for it hath work to do! Put it in the scullery at night, for I have seen a rat in there. They venture through the broken bricks. But do not tell a soul.'

'No madam.'

'I can no longer stay, Peg, but 'twas was worth everything to save this little boy from the pest-house. Look after him well and I shall be back when I can… Do not let him go to the gate and look into the lane, for the priest may be going to the market square and ask about him.'

'No madam.'

Jessica watched Jacob climbing about on the fallen tree by the shed: 'He may play there, by the shed, for it is hidden from the lane. How doth our new gardener?'

'He is grateful and works hard, madam. He hath been digging potatoes, and still doth tend to the roses and wonder why they cannot bloom.'

'He is risen?'

'Nay, madam, 'tis early yet.'

'I did forget. I see by the sundial, 'tis not yet seven-of-the-clock. Tell him I shall speak with him anon. For the child, if ye can sew up his sleeves to fit and wash his breeches, I would be glad.'

'Ay, madam.'

From the tail of her eye, Jessica caught Peg making a face in a careless manner. She reprimanded her: 'What have I told thee about unspoken insolence, Peg? I have looked after thee where I could have turned thee out of doors or sent thee to the pest-house. I shall not aby it.'

'For that I do be sorry, madam.'

'Think on, Peg.'

'Ay, madam.'

'I can no longer stay,' she told Jacob, 'for I have work to do, but I shall come again – and 'twill be soon.'

'Can I play with the cat?' he asked.

'Ay, but be sure he doth not venture, and 'twill be brought in at eventide to catch rats.'

As she left the house to return to the doctor's, Jessica stopped to look at the roses that hung down by the gate. Most of them were still in bud, but one had struggled to burst into blossom. She picked it but saw that it had crumbled – and died at its hour of birth.

25

The doctor wasn't at home when Jessica arrived, but had left evidence to suggest that he had been busy putting his surgical skills to good use. Surgery was crude and painful for its victims then, but the kindly doctor ensured that his charges had a good glass of brandy before he set to work on them to the repeating tune: 'This will not hurt.' The evidence included lancets and wads of bloody cotton wool which had been put into in a wooden bowl after use. This, and other evidence, had been placed on a table beside the bed. As she approached, Jessica was suddenly aghast, for hanging from the bed near to the floor, with an expression somewhere between terror and amazement, was a poor old woman with dressings by her arm-pits and on her neck. She burned with fever and was covered in vomit. 'Oh, my dear Lord!' she exclaimed.

There was an ungodly stench around the woman and Jessica stood horrified. She had been prepared to mop brows and hold the hands of the sick, to speak gently to them and perhaps apply a dressing but was not prepared for this. It was then that the woman cried – such a desperate cry – that surely would awaken compassion in the hardest heart. Jessica drew near to her and the woman clutched at her with a pleading that went deeper than words. A lump appeared suddenly in Jessica's throat and she clasped the woman's hand.

'I am a sinner. I am a sinner, and God hath struck me down…' the woman repeated in breathless tones.

'Ye are not a sinner,' insisted Jessica, wiping her face,

'for the good Lord...' But she could comfort her no more, for the woman sighed away her last breath.

Jessica sat by the bed-side for some while, wondering at the wisdom of letting blood and lancing boils when the poor soul was so sick. 'Why should she have endured more pain?' she wondered. She knew that the doctor meant well and had hoped to save her life, but the poor soul was beyond saving. She could have cried but didn't, for crying was a waste of time. Rolling up her sleeves, she set to work to wash the battered body – and everything that stank around her.

The doctor had gone to get more dressings from the apothecary in the market square, but found the door locked and bolted against him. The apothecary had fled – along with all the other apothecaries nearby. Chagrined, he made his way back along the alley and came across James kneeling in prayer, a dying man propped up beside him by the wall. James had adopted a certain courage now, and was no longer wary of catching the plague.

'How now, James?'

'Good morrow, doctor – if the morrow be good.'

'It is not.' The doctor stooped and felt a pulse. 'He hath gone to his maker,' he said, closing the victim's eyes. 'Oh, I am tired of it, James, tired of it!'

'Ay, I do feel my soul sink.'

The doctor waited, in respect for James to finish a prayer, then said, 'The apothecary hath gone.'

'Nay!'

'I have little left to dress the wounds...'

'Constables, watchmen, all taken – and the devil rides unchallenged,' said James. 'Ah, he comes!'

The sound of the bell came closer so they stepped away from the alley. From a distance they witnessed the dead man taken up, flung into the cart and trundled off with a heap of others.

'Is there no blessing?' said James.

'There is a small blessing – for there is not a quack left in London Town to testify to the success of his ill-begotten remedies, and 'tis a blessing, indeed.'

'Justice divine!' said James, spreading his hands to the sky. 'What news abroad?'

'Lately I did hear from Sir John. The poor wretches they do call "the useless mouths" and servants turned out of doors, do gather in multitudes upon Bunhill Fields and further hence. Some poor dear souls are near starvation. Others are with pestilence struck down and drag themselves in bushes so to die. Oh, 'tis a woe that haunts my dreams.'

'A terrible sight that I care to think not of.'

'Ay, 'tis best, James. Methought I was inured – not to harden my heart, but...'

'Ay, 'tis impossible, said James.'

'Yet we must stay firm to the purpose, for surely these evil vapours cannot last forever.'

James laid his hand on his friend's shoulder. 'Ye are a goodly strength to us all.'

'Nay, my strength begins to wane. I am a sot. By day I venture forth only if I drink. If I am fortunate to sleep by night – Oh, God – by night! My nightmares they do come thick and fast. I dream they do gather round the pits –

poor pitiful souls – and they do cry for help to a God who hears them not.'

'Horrible!'

'Then the insects flee the dead in a plaguy mass and looking for living flesh, assail me. Then – and this repeats night after night – up in a puff of smoke to compound all ills, doth come Jack Hogg!'

'The devil! Doctor, ye are overworked. Ye scarce can have time for dreams. It will be well to ask Sir John for help.'

'Nay, he is sunk. The faster he doth run to catch this monster, the faster it doth overtake him.' He swayed. 'I must have physic,' he said, gulping it back.

'Perchance there is one left in London Town – not of the College for ye say there are none – yet someone with mettle.'

'Nay – My friend who doth sniff the breath is without the parish, and doth struggle the same as I. This is it that assists me,' he said indulging further.

'Nay, do not drink the spirit doctor, for it shall make thee ill.'

'Yet it hath repelled the plague. I tell ye it doth work mag – magic,' he said in a slur.

'It doth work on thy tongue to confuse it – and on thy legs – for one goes north, the other south.'

'And I know not where I go. I can go no further today, James. Would I could lie down and let the devil take what little is left of my humanity.'

'Ye cannot give up. There is yet something we can do – if we durst do it,' he said carefully. 'For it may awake derision and hurt our pride.'

'What durst we do? The physicians are all gone, and I am alone in the parish.'

James paused, then said tentatively: 'The lady Jessica is the one.'

'Jessica? Not four and twenty hours ago ye did dismiss her,' complained the doctor.

'I was wrong. I have thought of nothing since. I know that she could help.'

'We told her nay.'

'Ay, yet I own it was a mistake. Ye would lose face so too would I, but I know we did mistake. Jessica is strong and hath a brain. She could do much.'

'Nay, I do not trust thy reasoning. Ye are love-struck and she doth cloud thy judgement.'

'Not so. I judge her obstinate, impertinent, contrary – yet she is clever. A round or two with her and I am out.'

'By this, ye would have me the nurse and thy lady the physician,' said the doctor.

'Ay, 'tis true,' James agreed. 'Yet think ye, doctor… How fares the new nurse-keeper?'

'She doth belie her lowly looks, for she hath challenged my authority.'

'A low nurse-keeper challenged thee?' he chuckled.

'Ay – She may do well, if she ceases her mischief.'

'There is an echo in it.'

'She doth work uncommon hard.'

'Then that is good,' said James, 'yet I do urge thee to consider...'

'Jessica? Nay, nay. She must not face the plague. I alone must carry on. But I can no longer parley, James.'

'Nor I. I shall go with thee to thy door, my friend –

and do entreat thee to drink no more.'

The doctor arrived at his house to discover that all that he had left in disarray was now in order. The new nurse-keeper was hard at work, scrubbing the blood off the floor, and she looked up when he came in. She saw that he was swaying this way and that, struggling to stand still.

'Ye must lie down and rest, sir,' she said, 'for I declare that ye have done the work of a dozen physicians.'

'For a dozen of the wretches – nay more – turned tail and fled the town. Now the apothecary in the alley hath followed on their heels, I have little left to dress the wounds...Oh, I do tire.'

'I shall help the housemaid to cut up old linen for dressings. Now rest ye, doctor. I can attend to thy work while ye do sleep.'

'Ay,' said the doctor in a stupor, unaware what he'd agreed to.

As he lay back and closed his eyes the housemaid knocked and came in, bringing the examiner with her, but the doctor didn't stir. 'A family in Duck Alley need the doctor, for the man doth cry in pain,' he demanded.

'The doctor hath worked six and twenty hours and is spent,' said Jessica. 'He bid me attend.'

'A nurse-keeper?' The examiner eyed the girl doubtfully.

'I bid thee wake him and ask, or wait till the morrow when he hath slept – 'tis all one. I did but offer to help.'

The examiner peered at the doctor. 'He is snoring like a hog and they do need some physic now,' he insisted.

'Then 'tis tomorrow,' said Jessica, 'for he cannot be woken.'

'Have ye physic?' asked the examiner, with a shade of suspicion.

'I shall get it,' said Jessica, and soon returned with a filled basket.

'Ye must make haste,' he said.

They followed the sound of whimpering up a flight of worn steps hewn a century ago. They led to a hovel in Duck Alley, where the door opened to reveal a poor family – five of them crammed into one filthy room – the father in great pain, the mother weeping over him and the children huddled in the corner.

'Do what ye can,' ordered the examiner, thrusting a scented kerchief beneath his nose, and as he left the house he let in the searcher. The searcher, intent on seeking out the dead, began poking and prodding at the father with her stick. He cried out in pain, his family taking up the cry in witness to it.

'Desist!' cried Jessica. 'Do not do that! He is not yet taken. What use are ye? Go to, and let me give him physic,' she demanded. 'Ye shall not behave thus.'

'Ye speak like a gentlewoman. What doth a lady here?' asked the searcher.

'What she will. Shall not a lady nurse the sick?'

'The lady shall be taken – along with the likes of me,' said the searcher.

'Nay, for the lady hath good purpose,' said Jessica.

'Bah, I would give thee for a witch,' spat the searcher.

'Then ye may vanish in a puff of smoke – for I have work to do.' She was afraid of no-one.

Jessica watched her go, then knelt down beside the labourer. 'What means this? I see no boils or blotches on thy husband.' She felt his brow. 'He hath no fever, thus no plague.' She looked grave, and placing her fingers upon his neck, added: 'Yet it is not well.' Suddenly, the man raised himself towards her, reached out as though in plea, and with a groan fell back. Jessica put her fingers on his neck again and said: 'His heart hath stopped at once!' And with a dreadful wail, his wife fell down beside him in despair and the children gathered round and sobbed. Jessica fetched her basket of remedies, put it down beside them and turning to the woman said: 'Cry no more. Thy husband is with God. Can he be in greater care? Now ye must tend to thy children.'

'How tend them when I have nothing?' asked the sobbing woman.

'Ye shall have alms. But first, I have some good physic for thee.' She passed round a jug of honied milk and let them drink. 'Here are herbs – wild garlic is the best. I leave ye potatoes and some wheaten bread.'

The children said little all the while, for they were so shaken by their father's death, but by turns began to pick hungrily at the bread.

'What are thy names?' asked Jessica.

The tallest – a girl of about nine years – stood up, wiped her moist nose with the back of her hand and punctuated each name with a sob. 'Mary. This be John and – and Beth...' Just as they gathered near, there came a loud clanging in the street below, followed by the deathly call of the dead-carter, discordant, cutting into the peace that had at last begun to descend on them.

'No!' cried the woman.

'Remember. He is with God,' Jessica said quickly.

Suddenly the priest appeared from the shadows.

'James!' Eyes wide, she gasped and covered her mouth in the shock of exposing her identity. But he had already discovered her by the authority in her voice, leaving her disguise worthless. She stood silently aside, pulse racing, as he gathered the family together in prayer. But the prayer was rudely ended by a loud banging on the door and the searcher pushed her way in.

'Ye durst not tarry. The cart be waiting,' she said, insensitive to the children's pleas, and their poor mother's protestations as she clung to a lifeless body – yet warm.

'Out of the door!' said James, rising. 'How dare ye interrupt the sanctity of prayer?'

'Jack won't wait.'

'Jack will wait – until the morrow,' said James.

'Till the morrow? Ye shall feel his wrath!' warned the searcher.

'Then he shall feel the wrath of God – when the mayor shall clap him in the stocks,' countered James.

'And who'll wheel the dead cart then?'

As she turned tail and left, her footsteps could be heard retreating down the steps, along with a last clanging of the bell.

When James had finished the prayer, Jessica approached the sobbing woman gently, telling her: 'I bid thee farewell, but I shall keep my promise to arrange for alms.'

'I do thank thee – and my children thank thee – for all ye have done,' said the woman. 'Though I cannot repay thee.'

'I do not ask ye to,' said Jessica. 'Fare thee well.' And turning to James, said. 'Fare thee well, priest.'

'But wait!' he urged.

She hurried away, and he followed after her down the steps and into the alley. 'I wish to speak to thee,' he said.

'What is to say? Ye found me out.'

'Ay.'

'And now ye would tell the doctor of my trick?'

'Nay.'

'Nay? Then would ye dangle my disguise above my head?' She removed her linen cap and curls fell down about her shoulders.

'Nay.'

'Then laugh at me?'

'I would not laugh at thee, Jessica. This afternoon, I did tell the doctor we did mistake.'

'How so?' she asked, feigning petulance.

'I should have known, for I have seen thee with the sick before – tending the shop girl in the church porch. And moments since, I did testify again to thy ability.'

'Ye do condescend – for that thy friend is desperate for help.'

'I do not condescend.' He paused. 'Yet tell me, what mean potatoes and a wheaten loaf?' He laughed. 'They are not physic.'

'Ye laugh! And but a moment hence said ye would not. The potatoes and the wheaten loaf – do they not give faith and hope, and are they not charity? And are not this trinity part of physic?'

'Ye drive me in the hazard!'

'Ye drive me to love ye where I would not!'

Shocked at her confession, she turned and hurried along the alley to the doctor's house and pushing her curls under her linen cap, went in and closed the door.

26

It was the end of August, and the roses still refused to bloom. The citizens of London wondered whether they would ever see the end of the visitation that was claiming so many lives. The sun beat down increasing the stench – along with the fleas that insinuated themselves into clothes, into beds, into every filthy crevice. Yet the elusive wretches that caused the distemper could not be identified. Moreover, they were far from being the inhabitants of an imagined cloud, trailed in the wake of a shooting star that some citizens believed had augured disaster, but inhabited the black rats that fed upon the rubbish in the close-set streets, now host to the homeless and displaced...

As James came from the market square, he discovered a young 'prentice wandering sadly in the street.

'Good morrow, boy. What do ye do abroad? Do ye not fear the distemper?'

'No sir, I care not.'

'It hath pleased God to preserve ye. Will ye not be advised and shut thyself within doors?'

'I go to the grocer's, sir.'

'Ah. Is all well?'

'Nay. My family is all gone, and I do fear the loneliness more than I do fear the plague.'

'For that I am sorry. If ye do seek fellowship, there are a few such lonely souls that gather at yonder church. Go thee there, boy. By and by I shall come.'

'I thank thee, sir,' said the boy. 'I shall go,' and he

went his way to the market place. It was then that two young children ran from the alley, each crying out for their mother, and James hurried after them to protect them from the danger of the streets.

'Wherefore thy tears?'

'We do be lost.'

'We are alone…'

They wept, as children weep when losing the comfort of a mother's hand in a crowded place.

'They did take her in a cart,' said the elder of the two.

James was incredulous: 'And did leave ye all alone?'

'Ay.'

'The devil Jack Hogg!' and looking upwards he cried: 'Is there no justice beneath the sky?'

Not a moment later, Alf appeared suddenly from the alley: 'Jack's been taken with tokens and Doll be sick!'

'Providence!' whispered the priest and, seeing the 'prentice turn towards the direction of the church, said: 'Take these children with thee. There are goodly people there shall give thee sustenance. Anon I shall come.'

'Ay sir.'

James watched the 'prentice take the children by the hand and lead them towards the church. Then he stood a while, contemplating the archway, wrestling with his conscience, for Jack's hovel lay the other side of it. He had heard that Jack and Doll, the worst of them, were suffering as he had hoped they would suffer. Now, with a pang, he felt the need to pray with them – sinners or not. Making up his mind, he walked purposefully into the archway and beyond, to discover the two rogues – Doll gasping her last upon a stair, Jack crying out oaths terrible to hear. Beside them was a large barrow displaying the corpses of victims left hours under the sun and horrible to behold, and such was the hellish stench, that, nauseated, he raised his kerchief to his face and began to walk away. He had not gone a few yards when he heard Jack call out to him.

'Priest! Come, I prithee, for I am a sinner and have need of ye...'

James continued to walk away.

'Priest!' Jack called – 'Ye betray thy Lord!'

James stopped and turned. 'I should let ye burn in hell, Jack Hogg,' he said, but the outburst did not assuage his anger.

'I do be sorry for my sins,' cried Jack.

At that moment, James knew that he must say a prayer or defrock. 'Only at this late hour do ye repent?'

'Yet I do repent!'

James approached and knelt down to say a prayer beside the rogue who, with maniacal strength, suddenly pulled him down and held a knife to his throat. 'Remember, ye have been hated, priest!'

James had no time for fright, for the knife dropped to the ground and Jack was taken. Within a minute, Doll had followed him. A moment ago, it had seemed the hardest thing in the world to do good – so much easier to have thrown Jack's barbs back at him, kicking him while he lay helpless on the ground – serving him as he had served others for the best part of his miserable life. Instead, he struggled against all his retributive instincts and, kneeling down, did the work of a priest.

The prayer was almost unutterable and, as he rose to

go on his way, he was met by the bizarre sight of poor Alf swaying about, prompting an unruly clang of his bell and spinning in a grotesque semi-circle as he dropped to the ground, silencing the bell forever. This saddened the priest, for Alf, a victim of the wars tipped back into society penniless, had been the blameless victim of a hard life. James knelt down and a prayed with ease.

There was no-one left to drive the dead-cart, abuse the sick or clang the bell now. With a dearth of officers to maintain order in the vicinity and the threat of bodies rotting in the alleyways, James decided to get a message to the Lord Mayor. As he neared the doctor's house, he noticed him in the street outside his door and hailed.

'I need air, James, I need air!' gasped the doctor, mopping his brow. 'God, I...' He clutched at his neck cloth.

'Doctor, what ails thee? God forbid 'tis not the plague,' said James, hurrying to steady him.

'Nay, nay...Ha! It touches me not,' the doctor protested, huffing out alcohol on his breath. 'Nay, 'tis not the plague that ails me, but 'tis my body festers – 'tis my mind. I kill myself with this to stay alive,' he said, brandishing a bottle. He laughed hysterically at the paradox.

'God's mercy! These are hard times for us all. Come inside and lie ye down, sir, for ye must rest.'

'Yet there is none,' said the doctor as James led him into his house and sat him down. 'There is no rest...'

'Ye must listen, for 'tis of moment,' urged James. 'Jack Hogg, Doll and Alfred – all are taken.'

'Ay,' said the doctor, unimpassioned.

'The dead do hang about the streets unburied…'

Suddenly the doctor roused and said: 'What care I? My remedies fail as no better than the quack's, so the plague steals the people from me. How have I remained free of it? – By this.' He raised an empty bottle. 'I have no pestilence – but, oh! – never did my tears so swiftly fall to behold such tragic sights as I would banish from my eyes or else run mad…'

'Doctor!'

'Misery issues from every door – daughter wails for mother, mother for son, son for father and father for brother… all in an ill-harmony of caterwaul so long in mine ear that I should no longer truly care. This soul crouches in a corner dumbstruck, that soul from a casement hangs – breathing such malodorous, contaminated air that horror frights the gasping of it.'

James clasped his hands together: 'Again, I call on God…'

'Damn your God!' shouted the doctor.

'Lord forgive him – have mercy!'

But the doctor raved on: 'Damn him! Damn him, I say, for 'tis easier to dig up the fields of England with a spoon than quench this plague!' He sobbed. 'I am, sir, nothing, more than nothing.'

'Ye must rest,' said James. Rest thyself and preserve thy sanity.'

The doctor sat up straight. 'Nay, I am ashamed. I did lose control.'

James put a protective hand on the doctor's shoulder. 'If, as ye say, ye can do no more, then ye have done enough my friend. Betake thyself to bed and rest. I shall prevail upon the nurse-keeper to help thee.'

'Nay, nay, it cannot be done. She is but a girl,' protested the doctor. He paused and looked about him, and said at last: 'Insects – they are invisible and do crawl at night, for I have felt them. Mark me: 'tis they bring the pestilence – 'tis they I say,' and he collapsed in his chair – exhausted.

'What intend ye to do?' asked James.

'Do? I am the only physician within miles of this hell-hole, and I do waste my time in tears when I should be mopping brows and tending running sores.'

'Yet rest thee now. Where is the nurse-keeper?'

'She hath gone to a garden to harvest herbs. She hath been gone long.'

'I would speak with her.'

But there was no reply from the exhausted doctor and James turned to go. As he did so, the door opened and Jessica hurried in with a basket of herbs and gooseberries.

'Dear lady...' James whispered.

'James!'

'Ye have been long and the doctor hath need of thee.'

'I did but go to attend to my household and harvest herbs and gooseberries. I did promise the good doctor a pie. While I was there, I saw...'

'What saw ye Jess – Meg?' – asked James, conscious of the doctor's open eye.

'I was amazed at what I saw. The roses wither on their stems and die as though they sense the horror of it all. Some full-abloom fall down, and some do wither before their petals spread. Others – and 'tis this that did distress me – shrivel and die in bud like things that could have been.'

'They are but flowers – Meg.'

'Nay, they are reflections of this sad humanity.'

'Which ye reflect too long upon.'

'Nay. I wonder – Perchance the roses are afraid. Is thy God in such a rage that he doth fright the delicate roses out of bloom?'

'That is not my God, Jessica, and ye do know it.'

He moved towards her, but the doctor sat up suddenly and cried: 'Insects!'

'How insects?' Jessica wondered.

'They have the canker upon them,' insisted the doctor.

'There are no insects on my – those roses,' she insisted, 'for the gardener doth wash them away with soap.' She was beginning to forget her disguise.

'And none that I could see,' said James. 'Last evening, I did walk forth to take the air in the lane beside the church. I did mark the musk roses that did o'er hang a gate at the back of the big house. They were dun brown before the passing of their time. I saw no blackfly then, no cankerous enemy.'

'They do hide,' added the doctor, 'I tell thee they do hide...'

James took Jessica aside and said to her: 'The doctor hath roamed abroad distracted, Jessica. I would that ye could help him.'

'Ay. Yet 'tis not with fever that he burns, 'tis this,' she said, snatching the bottle from his grasp, 'but 'tis not for the nurse-keeper to tell him.'

'Of that I am aware,' said James, noting that the doctor had again fallen into a stupor and was snoring.

A shriek came suddenly through the open window.

'I shall to the sick. I have a basket of physic always waiting. Ye do dither, sir,' she said to James. 'Perchance I play the priest as well.'

'I shall not be told,' cut in the doctor, making no sense. But they had gone and closed the door.

27

With almost a third of Londoners in their graves, and the mass exodus of others that had fled in terror, there was an eerie quiet about the streets and alleys now. It was punctuated by a whimper or a cry made more potent in the soundless air. The shutting up of houses was no longer enforced, yet some citizens, who feared to walk abroad, now volunteered to imprison themselves in their homes, but like a phantom vapour, the plague followed them and wreathed around them as a serpent intent on crushing and consuming them.

The inebriate doctor was on the edge of collapse. He not only relied on the whisky to keep him safe from the plague, but to give him courage to cope with the terrible tasks that came his way each day. The cook had already left, seeking refuge with her sister in Bury St. Edmonds, and now the housemaid had fled. He was no longer a young man and could neither muster a meal nor keep his house in order. He came to rely more and more on the nurse-keeper, remembering that physicians in those days were obliged to carry out their own nursing duties. In this regard, Jessica was soon able to unburden him.

Sometimes, early in the morning or late at night when the doctor was in bed, Jessica would steal into the study to read anatomy and physiology, for she was convinced that a nurse-keeper – or nurse, as she preferred to be called – could do the job much better with the right kind of knowledge. One morning, she became absorbed in the findings of William Harvey.

'De Motu Cordis,' she already knew a little Latin. 'Ah,

the motion of the heart,' and she began to study Harvey's findings on the heart and the circulation of the blood. She had already learned something about the pulse, for from the beginning she had closely observed the doctor at his work and had surprised him by asking questions. Lately, she had been busy memorising all the major bones in the body and noting how they articulated – courtesy of a book of anatomy and the grim skeleton hanging by the door. Fascinated, she read on, and this particular morning she had let time run away with her, and the doctor came upon her unaware...

'Ah, the nurse-keeper – De Motu Cordis?' He queried as she quickly shut the tome.

'Ay – and uncommon dusty, sir,' she said, in the guise of Meg.

He shot a knowing look towards her. 'Do ye have the dressings that ye promised?'

'Ay, the housemaid did leave aprons in the chest and I did cut them up. Oh, and I did burn the filthy dressings that I found upon the floor.'

'Ah, 'tis well. I am in a muddle, Meg. Where are my instruments?'

'There is no muddle now. I did soak thy instruments in vinegar, for 'tis acid and doth clean them well.'

'I thank the Lord for thee.'

'And I did empty the filthy vomit – and did wash the wooden bowls and...'

'Ye are uncommon sensible.'

There came a knock on the door.

'Ah, 'tis the priest!'

'Sir.' Jessica acknowledged him with a bob and hastily

left the room. Already she felt that she had seemed too familiar with him, and more and more had let her guard down.

'I begin to suspect I could not do without my nurse-keeper,' said the doctor. 'She doth anticipate the needs of my profession. I should teach her to let blood, James!'

'I am sure she could let blood,' he said – partly to himself. 'She hath a spirit about her, doctor.'

'Ay.' The doctor circled the room without purpose. 'Oh, I have been in such a muddle, James, but Meg – she doth un-muddle me.'

'Then let – Meg – un-muddle thee more. The girl is as capable, is she not? Entrust her with more.'

'Ay, but I do suspect she is not so humble. See her smooth hands and aspect of gentility.'

'Nay – Ye do mistake, sir. She hath a dirty face and by that is indeed humble – but she is a goodly nurse-keeper.'

'Ay, I am blessed. Well, James, to the purpose. What did ye want?'

'Want? – Ah, I did come to get some more plague water.' He shuddered at his lie.

'More? Already gone? Nay, 'tis impossible.'

'I did spill it.' The lie choked him.

'Spill the plague water I did spend my time distilling?'

'I do repent me, doctor,' he said, finding it necessary also to repent his lies, 'and I do bid thee good morrow.'

In truth, James had hoped to speak to the nurse-keeper, but she busied herself in the kitchen. When she heard him go and close the door, she knocked and took the doctor broth. 'Now I am cook and nurse-keeper,' she said.

'Ye did tell me that ye could not cook. How so?'

'For that I wanted to nurse the sick, sir.'

'Ah.'

'But I cannot do the laundry, for I do only have two hands.'

'I shall tell Sir John, for I do swear he hath all the servants left in London Town. Ay, 'tis certain he will lend a laundrywoman. To the matter, Meg. I have been unwell of late and I need ye to help me more. It seems the doctor cannot cure himself. It is the priest advises me. On the morrow, when ye follow me on my rounds, will do what ye can?'

'Ay, doctor.'

The following day the doctor was drinking well before they set out on his rounds. Jessica was anxious and wanted to advise him, but as a humble nurse-keeper was not at liberty to do so.

'We must go thither,' he said. 'and I do warn thee, Meg, 'tis not pretty beneath the arch where chaos rules.'

'I do know, sir.'

'There is no order now. They do roam abroad distracted, and 'tis no use to lock the poor souls up – God! – to be the only physician here. What can I do? As fast as my hands do work, they must work faster and all for naught.'

Jessica could feel his despair. 'Nay, doctor, for ye have a nurse-keeper by thy side.'

'Ay – Yet more afflicted souls do gather pitifully beneath the arch. Now gather thy physic. We must go to them.'

'Ay, sir.'

'Are ye sure, Meg, for tis a tunnel of vapours?'

'I have lavender, doctor, and put my kerchief around my face…'

'And I do need thy help. First soak thy apron in vinegar. Bring garlic cloves, plague water, plasters – bring what ye will.'

'Ay – and fresh water from the well…'

'Fresh water?'

'For 'tis hot and they shall thirst and have the need to drink.'

'Ye have no time to go to the well.'

'I have it ready, sir, 'tis in the jug.'

'Make haste. Bring all the dressings ye hath. Too long do we tarry.'

'Ay, 'tis ready in the basket, sir.'

He looked at her, and with a look of recognition in his eye said: 'I am blessed in thee – but I would have thee wash they dirty face on the morrow.'

As they approached, the way was blocked by toppled boxes – some spilling produce over the cobbles and, as they picked their way past, a terrible stench of death emanated from the archway as though daring them to enter. Once in, the suffering of humanity in agony and despair was painful to witness. Surely, deep within the arch was hell itself? Some poor souls sat prostrate of the ground, some prone – their eyes wide with terror. Others cried and called to God and asked why he'd forsaken them. Some had stumbled unaware into this dreadful place, and had collapsed in shock, some dead, some barely alive, some scrambling away, all in a vaporous compound of effluence, sweat and pig dung. Some souls roused when the doctor came near, as though grasping at the air for a wisp of hope, and he was at once weighed down…

'I do not know where to start,' he said, 'for it doth overpower me.'

'What shall I do to help?' asked Jessica.

'Ye may…' he swayed, for he was well fortified with whisky.

'Help dress the wounds?' she asked.

'Ay, help dress the wounds.'

'But first,' she said, 'we must move the poor souls – already taken – out of the arch, for we do need room to work.'

'Ay, said the doctor,' tipsy with the drink, and together they lifted the bodies out of the archway. Then returning to the desperate souls within, the doctor began to apply a remedy of garlic, and dress the sores. 'I bid thee help me, Meg,' he said.

'Ay, but first I'll give them water. It is a common need,' and she knelt beside them one by one, and those who could, drank fresh water from the well.

The doctor turned and saw that a girl among them stood up.

'She stands,' said Jessica. 'She was not ill but had a thirst. What is thy name, girl?'

'Mary – I do be Mary.'

'The lord be praised,' the doctor said. 'Bid her wait by my house.'

For more than an hour, the doctor and his nurse-keeper laboured with the sick. For many of the souls it was too late, and palliative care was all they could give. Then, at the last, they moved them into the street beyond the arch to die.

'I cannot weep, I must not weep,' said Jessica.

'Ye learn well,' Meg,' said the doctor, 'for nothing is achieved with tears.' One escaped his eye.

'I shall put lavender about,' said Jessica, but the fragrance was overpowered, and it did nothing to stem the tide of stench.

'We can do no more. Now the priest must pray for souls,' said Jessica.

'Dear God, ye do my work!'

It was then that James came from prayers at a house in the market square. The market place that was once alive with activity, replete with street sellers and a shamble of pitiful animals crying out, was now deathly quiet – but for a wary fishmonger and grocer who shrank away from their customers, proffering pots of vinegar to receive their coins. The filthy street was almost impassable now that the raker had gone, but James made a determined way through to the archway to comfort what souls he could.

'Our work is finished,' said the doctor, 'and I see the priest is come.'

'And I shall go,' said Jessica quickly, 'for the girl is waiting at thy house, sir.'

'Ay,' said the doctor, 'and I do thank thee, Meg, for the help ye have given.'

'I am glad to help thee,' she said, and turning to James: 'Good morrow, priest.'

'Good morrow – to ye,' he replied, and watched her worn figure turn from the alley to the doctor's house. 'The nurse-keeper was of help to thee?' he asked.

'An angel fallen from heaven, sir! I did wonder if I was physician or the nurse-keeper. Good morrow, James.' He chuckled, supped and went his way.

To suspend disbelief and walk among those streets at that time, brings with it a dreadful sense of horror and despair. Yet such as the good doctor, the priest and the nurse-keeper, are surely reflections of the few who cared for humanity then. It is true that, however ill a person may be, whatever their status, they should be able to take leave of the world in peace and dignity. That is what the nurse-keeper hoped to achieve – sometimes against all odds.

28

September passed and the worst of the plague seemed to be abating. Slowly, people began to go about their business in the usual way. Some, who had faced near starvation, came back from the country – hoping to start earning a living again. It was unwise, for the plague was not yet over and like the eye of a storm stirs a destructive wind in its wake, so malign pockets of plague surfaced again at random, killing yet more unsuspecting citizens, many of whom had believed themselves to be preserved. Some were wise enough to bide their time – including those who had gone much further afield. Coach journeys were long and arduous, and families were not prepared to travel all the way back to London unless they knew for certain it was safe. For those who had stayed behind to weather the storm, it was as though they were being played with by a puppeteer God – who offered them hope, only to toss them back again into the thick of it.

The elderly doctor, who had drunk his way throughout the crisis, had certainly justified his method by remaining clear of the infection but, as the plague subsided, he decided to break the habit – the alcohol taking its toll on his health. James, who had had his faith tested time and time again, due to his diminished congregation, had rolled up his sleeves and made himself available to the doctor and to the nurse-keeper. For the nurse-keeper, she thrived on hard work. She stayed at the doctor's house then, and rarely had the time to visit her household, leaving Jacob in the care of

Peg and Thomas.

'I do need to get some apples,' she said. 'There are no more gooseberries left but apples in abundance. I shall not be long, doctor. All thy instruments are prepared and dressings ready for ye to use.'

'Make haste, Meg, for there is still much work to do.'

'Ay, but I do need apples for a pie, sir.'

On her arrival at her house, Jessica was at once hailed by Thomas running from the shed. 'Madam! Madam!'

'The matter?'

'The maid did run about distracted, and the boy did run out of the house...'

'Whither?'

'In the shed with the cat, madam. He was affrighted.'

'Yet when?'

'Yesternight. She ran about as from the devil, screamed and we heard her no more.'

'Whither now? She is within?'

'Ay, madam – plague-struck.'

'Plague-struck – Peg?'

'Ay, madam – I do think she is dead.'

'Dead? Nay, not Peg.'

Jessica stood silent for a while, breathing slowly. That vital little person taken – Peg? She could not credit it. 'I must go to her and make her well,' she said. 'I shall come to Jacob anon. First, I must go into the house.'

'Ay, madam.'

Jessica stepped warily inside. Treading slowly and looking to the ground, she saw a trail of ribbons, fans and fripperies – as though someone had tipped the contents of her little chest down the stairs. She followed the trail and climbed carefully to the landing. Whether the stairs or the wainscoting had creaked as she gripped the bannister, she was unsure but it seemed as though the sound was mocking her, telling her that all was not well. Her bedroom door was ajar, inviting her in. Before her, lying across her bed, was a most horrible sight. It was Peg, her maid, swathed in the silk of one of Jessica's dresses, her face made-up carelessly like a mask, her eyes staring as though startled by the tokens that gathered down the side of her neck. Jessica stood covering her mouth. Of all the ill forms she has seen while she worked as nurse-keeper, surely this was the worst: a grotesque figure of a person mocking her from the grave, a figure who had once been her friend. With a sharp breath, she turned and fled downstairs into the garden.

As she leant against the garden wall to catch her breath, she heard singing. The boy, Jacob, was entertaining the gardener with folk-songs in an effort to keep his spirits up. Jessica listened, and the tuneful lyrics floated out like balm upon the air.

'How beautifully he sings,' she said. 'I do think he should join a choir after the plague is over.' Her words were somehow at odds with the horror of it. 'But to the matter, I am sorry to say that Peg has been taken. Tell me – What did she do while I was gone?'

'Changed with the moon, madam. She did strut about wearing thy silks and jewels and did order us about like her servants. I did not fret for myself but for the boy, for she would neither cook for him nor clean his clothes and did jibe at him all the time that he would catch the plague.'

'Monstrous!'

'A while since, before ye came, she chased the screaming boy and I did shut him in the shed – and there we stayed until ye came, for she did threaten us with the vapours.'

'Wicked girl! – Yet we must pardon her for she knew not what she did in her affliction.

'Ay, madam.'

'I shall send...' She hesitated and said beneath her breath: 'I do not wish to speak of the cart – for that the boy may overhear. I shall send someone to the house to make arrangements, and a girl to help ye,' she promised. 'She is yet young but she would work. Her name is Mary.... Have ye eaten?'

'Ay,' said the gardener. 'I did bake potatoes in a fire, and we did eat apples.'

'I am glad. There is salt-fish in the pantry, and I shall send broth and a wheaten loaf with the girl. She shall cook thee simple food. Oh, 'tis so hot,' she said.

There was a spring trickling into the garden. Many of the springs and ditches about the town were little less than open cesspools, harbouring typhus, the spotted fever and other waterborne diseases, but Jessica's spring gurgled fresh from the field nearby and had been culverted by the lane. She crouched down, wetted her apron and flannelled her face. 'Ah, 'tis cooler.'

'Ay,' said the gardener. 'Ye have had a shock.'

'So too have thee, Thomas. I am sorry I was not here. Please forgive me for being so long away, 'tis the work I do,' she continued. 'It doth keep me from my household...'

'Nay, madam, for we are ever grateful to ye. Do not worry about the boy, for he be safe with me,' said Thomas kindly.

'That I know,' she said. 'There are soft covers in the house – above the linen chest.'

'I shall seek them out, for he durst not stay inside,' said the gardener.

'How is the boy now?'

'Tired, madam. I think that he shall sing himself to sleep.'

'Bless the child.'

'He hath put a box in the shed,' said Thomas, 'and sleeps beside the cat – and sings to it, and it hath not left his side.'

'The cat is comfort, and his songs do charm away the plague,' she said.

'Ay, madam. He is a goodly lad,' said Thomas. 'He doth help me in the garden.'

'What of the roses?' she asked, walking towards the gate and sliding one between her fingers.

'They still be sick,' he said.

'Ay, 'tis a sadness. I shall ask the priest to send the sexton to collect the maid – he is but across the way by the graveyard. Ah, 'tis sad, for she was once a goodly soul. It seems the plague did make her mad.'

'Ay.'

'Ye are happy to be a gardener and not a saddle-maker?' she asked, stopping by the gate and admiring the newly-dug ground, the neat rows of cabbages and potatoes, the plant-pots filled with seedlings – evidence of his industry. 'I am glad to see ye look so well.'

'Ay' he said, 'I do like to watch things grow – but the crows did steel my peas.'

She laughed lightly. 'Then we shall starve! I bid thee stay as long as ye will to tend my garden.'

'I thank thee for thy charity, madam.'

'Nay, 'tis not charity. But I tarry, and must hasten on my way, for the doctor waits. I shall be here again anon.'

'Good even, madam.'

'Good even, Thomas. Oh, but I did forget the apples!' She took the bag and hurried down the lane – forgetting to dirty her face.

29

Autumn came with the reminder that the citizens of London had been falling down like leaves from a tree and, with the change of season, there were signs that the plague was abating. Gradually, those who had fled began to return to their homes, anxious to resume their affairs, take up their jobs again, busy themselves and re-start the wheels of commerce. For many, the foray into the countryside and beyond had been an ordeal. Naturally, they had not been welcomed in many of the little towns and villages round about, for fear that they carried with them the plague. Moreover, life was surely hard for the poor who had sought refuge in the outlying fields with little recourse to food and shelter. Now, as the winter was on its way, and news had spread that the death-rate had dwindled, many of the exiles returned home. While in London Town, some of those who had remained to see out the evil visitation, grew impatient with the strictures placed upon them and recklessly sought fun. For the doctor and his nurse-keeper, the lull – albeit dangerous – had given them a measure of respite…

One afternoon, the doctor looked up from his book: 'Galen had much to say. Did he not? I see ye have been reading it,' he said, prompting a surge of adrenaline for Jessica. 'Did ye think I was a numbskull – Jessica?'

'Nay, never, doctor – nothing but that ye were – are – a goodly, clever soul,' she said, her face flushed. 'I did but want to help. Oh, lord, I should not have washed my face!'

The doctor laughed heartily. 'Wash thy face? Nay, no dirt could hide the naughty dimple in thy cheek.'

'Ye did discover my disguise?'

'I think I did know thee from the start.'

'I know not what to say.'

'Then do not say it.'

'Yet I do have something to say...'

'Ah, 'tis more like the lady Jessica.'

Now that he knew her secret, Jessica was relieved to tell the doctor all about Thomas the gardener, little Jacob and the awful incident that had recently occurred at her house.

'Ye have had thy hands full,' he said, 'and still ye studied!'

'Only a little,' she said. 'But if I could study in Oxford as ye...'

'Nay, Jessica, 'tis not possible. Such study is a bar to thee,' he said. 'For that I am sad.'

'I do know it,' she resolved.

'Ay. Now, if ye would come with me, we are late upon our rounds. Yet, I'll warrant, there will be little need for physic. God willing the plague is all but gone, though we must be vigilant, for still the insects hide.'

'Ay, the beast may roar its last,' she agreed.

Jessica gathered up her basket and followed the doctor to a lane beside the inn. As they passed the inn-yard, they noticed a large group of citizens – shouting, tippling and roaring with laughter. Some wrestled, some played quoits, some rolled the dice, some played sleight-of-hand with a pea beneath a cup, and one played on a pipe, and all the while the ale flowed freely. All were merry-making – careless of the vapours.

'The mischief!' exclaimed the doctor. 'They do think the plague hath gone away, but it hath not. Still it lurks in the air and on the breath, and here they gather together to spread it – neighbour killing neighbour – and burden us withal. I shall not aby it.'

'Do not meddle, doctor, for they are drunk with ale and may rise up against ye,' warned Jessica.

'Yet there is no watch, no constable in sight – 'tis meet they should be told…'

'Nay, doctor!'

She was aghast, for the doctor would not listen. She watched in disbelief as he strode into the middle of the yard, upturned a stout wooden crate and stood on it. At the spectacle, the merry-makers gradually stopped their activities. Tankards were put down, and the pipe whistled and stopped mid-tune… They waited expectantly.

'Go ye home!' cried the doctor. 'Do ye not know that ye may catch the plague?'

There came a mumbling of discontent. 'Nay, 'tis gone,' said one. 'Only three buried in a week,' said another.

'I tell thee, the infection is still among us, and 'tis wise to keep apart and not cavort in crowds…' continued the doctor.

'Nay, we'll have none of thy plague…' and the discontent rumbled and grew.

'But still it lingers and shall spread, I tell thee,' cried the doctor.

'Quack!' someone cried, to peals of laughter, and

repeated the sound of a duck: 'Quack, quack, quack!'

The doctor was livid. 'I am no quack. I am a member of the Royal College of Physicians...'

But the shameful merry-makers were having none of it, and Jessica could bear it no longer. 'Doctor, doctor, come away!'

'But I have worked – I was the only one...'

'I know, doctor, but please...'

It was too late. One arrogant reveller removed the doctor's periwig with the aid of a sharp stick and, balancing it on the tip, held it aloft in victory. A cry went up, as though he had lost his head, leaving the doctor standing there with his noddle bare and his humiliation complete. It was too much for Jessica to endure.

'Give me that periwig!' She snatched it away and turned on them. 'What kind of citizens are ye, that ye have scorned the good doctor who hath toiled for the people of London Town since springtime without rest, and ye taunt him for play? I tell ye this: the ill vapours that hang over London Town, hang here yet – so too will ye, if he is harmed...' She could not believe the violence of her words.

'The lady is right.' James stood at the back of the yard. 'I vow, as a man of the cloth, to see ye punished, all, if ye do not return to thy homes.'

At the sight of the priest, they mumbled and dispersed.

Jessica arranged the doctor's periwig, and he gripped her hand in silent gratitude. 'Go ye home, doctor, she said. I shall to the house to attend to the dressings, for I do have the physic here. Go ye home and rest.'

'Ay,'

'I shall not be long, for there is little to do.'

'Yet 'tis a pause before another storm,' the doctor said, and made his way back to his house.

She turned to James. 'What ails ye?'

'I am spent. Oh, Lord, it pleases Providence to save me, an insubstantial fool who knows not what to do or say...'

'Ye said well by the inn.'

'Nay. I look at thee, Jessica, and I am naught.'

'Do not say it.'

In a sudden apostrophe to Heaven he cried out: 'Hither – come strike me down with a bolt of thy almighty lightning before I live to spend another worthless minute, who am thy worthless servant!'

'James!'

'I am spent.'

'Are ye sick?'

But the priest cringed, as though caught blaspheming: 'God!'

'Nay, do not be afeared – but tell me thy concern.'

'I have heard lamentations long and loud. Such sights! I ne'er knew the sharp stab of compassion ere today.'

'Then there is yet hope for thee. Tell me what ye saw.'

'The plague hath left chaos in its wake. I walked abroad – through Bell Alley and out upon the south side of St. James's. A sorrier more dismal sight I ne'er beheld. To see the poor ragged creatures begging alms: that one crawling upon his belly, this one covered in unholy sores and crying: "God, please forgive me if I have sinned!" He

179

did grovel to my God, and never did miscreant, dangling and dancing above the gallows, peep out with such a pleading eye for mercy. He was afeared of Hell.'

Jessica reached out to comfort him: 'What greater hell than this?'

'Ye do speak of mysteries, Jessica.'

'I am out of my time, James.'

'I fear ye despise me.'

'Nay, I do respect thee.'

'Respect one as weak as I?'

'Oh, James, I thought ye would have turned tail and run away like a rat long since, for ye were so afraid.'

'Because I was a coward.'

'Nay. Because ye stayed although ye were afraid. Ye stayed though ye could do naught for the poor souls who cried out for the infinite mercy of thy uncaring God, though ye knew thy God was treacherous…'

'No!'

'Thy merciless God…'

'Cease this!'

'Ye stayed, though ye trembled to do it, because ye needs must find out who and what ye are – and what ye truly believe. Ye are more afraid of thy merciless God than the pestilence.'

'Lady!'

'Ay – I durst speak out. How can ye make thy allegiance to such a wretched hard-hearted God of wrath?'

'Have ye no fear?'

'Nay – and neither should ye, James.'

'I am confused,' he said. He turned and rested his

head in his hands.

'Do not despair,' said Jessica kindly. 'We are all tired of it, but it cannot last forever.'

But the doctor had been right. Cases of the plague were increasing again, taking revenge on some of the unfortunate souls who had returned from the fields too early, and again there was much work to do.

30

After the loss of Peg, Mary, the thirsty young girl found destitute in the alley, had been grateful to work as maid in Jessica's household. She was given a small bed in the house-keeper's room in return for producing broth and going daily to the bakehouse for wheaten bread. Although charged with the care of little Jacob, he didn't trouble her much. Already he had adopted Thomas the gardener as his grandfather, to mutual satisfaction, because they had both lost their families to the plague. The shed they lived in was less like a shack and more like a large brick outhouse with a window. Such was the division in living conditions at that time, that the shed was far bigger than the thatched hovel in the field by the lane.

Mary was fifteen years old and, in gratitude to the mistress who had rescued her from a terrible fate, she was hard-working and more trustworthy than poor Peg was. Knowing that her household was in good hands, enabled Jessica to carry out her work as nurse-keeper and study, unimpeded by distracting domestic problems such as Peg had seen fit to present her with.

Now that her secret was out, Jessica had asked James to call at her house through her garden daily on the way from the church to ensure that all was well. This he was pleased to do, for it was an opportunity to enlarge his congregation which, overcrowded at the beginning of the plague, now had a deal of empty pews. It was on such a visit that he was alerted that all was not right in Jessica's household.

'Reverend, sir!' called Thomas, who had waited expectantly for the visit. 'We had not seen the maid with our broth today and I did find her sick.'

'How sick?' James tingled with fear, bearing in mind that there were still pockets of plague intent on doing their worst.

'I do not know sir. She had a fever and I did not wish to infect the boy.'

'Ye were wise,' said James. 'I shall hasten to the doctor and he shall come anon.'

'I thank ye, sir,' said Thomas, 'and do beg the doctor hasten hither.'

James hurried down Church Lane and across the square to the doctor's house, but the doctor was out dressing sores beyond the alleyway when he arrived. Instead, his pious heart missed a beat to find Jessica immersed in a book about the medicinal properties of herbs, hoping to enlarge her physic garden. She looked up suddenly on his arrival and, on hearing the news, closed the book with a thud. She grabbed her basket of physic and put on her cloak, for it was chilly autumn now.

'I do thank thee and bid thee tell the doctor on his return,' she said. She turned to go, then astounded him, for she hurried back and kissed him on the cheek before disappearing from the door.

'Dear God, she hath kissed me!' he whispered – with a blush.

Mary was feverish but coherent when Jessica arrived. 'Madam – I do be sorry...'

'Wherefore?' asked Jessica, kneeling down with her basket.

'For that I could not make the broth today,' said the girl.

'Oh, you poor child. The broth can wait. Thomas hath salt-fish, and potatoes and turnips cooking on his garden fire…'

'Ay, 'tis good.'

'So ye must not fret. Are ye hungry?'

'Nay.'

'Tell me, what ails thee?'

'I am hot.'

'And have a fever – thus ye must drink much to clear thy blood.' She took jug of water from her basket and said: 'Here. Drink all ye are able. See, 'tis well water – so by that, it doth make thee well.'

Mary drank gratefully, savouring each drop. 'It doth remind me of the archway,' she said.

'And that did make thee well. It was the same well water.'

Mary laughed weakly, and asked: 'Shall I die, madam?'

'I shall not let thee. Together we shall not let thee. Drink all ye can, Mary,' and again Mary drank.

'Do I have the plague?' she asked fearfully.

Jessica drew aside the girl's blouse to reveal her chest, but other than a slight heat-rash, there were no visible signs of the distemper. 'Do ye have any boils, lumps or sores – or any pain here?' She pressed the pit of the girl's arm.

'Nay, madam.'

'I am not a physician but, God willing, ye do not have the plague – or if it be so, 'tis only mild,' she said. 'I must get more water from the kitchen pump.'

When she returned, she began to mop Mary's sweating brow with a flannel. As she did so, the doctor appeared together with a capacious bag.

'I am come,' he said, breathlessly. 'The priest did catch me by a minute.' Jessica stood aside, to allow him to examine the patient. 'How doth she, Jessica?'

'She is more comfortable, doctor. I do not think she hath the plague.'

'Oft times it lurks yet doth not show itself,' said the doctor. 'For that I must let blood.'

'Nay, doctor, nay,' said Jessica, anxiously. 'I do not think ye need to. Galen hath argued with Hippocrates that letting blood is wrong.'

'Come, come, Jessica,' he said, 'Ye are the nurse-keeper, I am the physician.'

'I do beg thy pardon, doctor. I did not wish to presume.'

Genial though the doctor was, he had always taken great pride in his association with the Royal College of Physicians, and constantly asserted his authority. 'Then do not presume,' he said, withdrawing a lancet and bowl from the bag.

Mary began to cry.

'Doctor, the girl is afeared,' said Jessica.

Although she had no logical explanation, she knew intuitively that the procedure was wrong, and her reading of Galen had supported her. Her heart sank when the doctor prepared to incise the girl's tiny arm to withdraw her blood. It had not been wise to challenge his authority, so Jessica decided that the best way to change his mind would be to flatter him. An opportunity arose when the hand that held the knife began to quiver – courtesy of excessive alcohol.

'Thy mixture of garlic and milk hath been of great use, doctor,' she said hurriedly, 'the milk sustaining, and the garlic the best cleanser of blood that I have seen. I have seen the sick recover well with its skilful use. Would ye like to try thy remedy again?'

He put the lancet down on the table. Jessica had disarmed him. 'Have ye any?'

'Prepared in the kitchen, sir.'

Mary looked anxiously from one to the other.

'Ah, 'tis well,' he said, maintaining his authority, 'for the girl's arm is very tiny – 'tis smaller than the knife! I have, myself, been thinking for some time about the wisdom of depleting a patient's blood. Perchance I should try the milk and garlic.'

Jessica sighed with relief. 'I carry a bottle in my basket – knowing how ye trust the remedy,' she said.

'Ah, 'tis good,' said the doctor. 'Let me administer it.'

Soon after she drank, Mary slept and the doctor asked Jessica to tend her through the night.

'Ye are a goodly nurse,' he said to her, 'the best in London Town – for all else are villains – but ye are no more than a child. Do not get above thyself.'

'A child, doctor? I do intend to get above myself, for I am one-and-twenty years old on the day after the morrow,' she said, 'and thus I am of age.'

'Well, well, we must celebrate,' he said, 'for on thy

birthday, 'tis a goodly glass of wine, accompanied by my best cheese. What say ye?'

'And an apple pie. Yet we must celebrate at my house, doctor, for I shall not leave the patient – yet 'twill not be long before she is recovered.'

'Ay. Then I bid ye good day and shall come hither the day after tomorrow even with the priest. I do have few sick to tend today. If the girl should wake, give her a few drops of valerian to calm her down,' he said, producing a small glass phial from his pocket.

'I am glad,' said Jessica, 'for valerian is a goodly medicine.'

She sat by Mary's bed throughout the night nursing her and nodding, intermittently, until the cock crowed in the early morning. It was then that the girl sat up and, although still moist with sweat, declared that she felt much better.

'Thank the Lord!' said Jessica. 'On my birthday, ye shall hear me play the lute.'

31

Winter came suddenly with a bitter howl, bringing back to London a reduced number of citizens who had been living rough in the nearby forests and fields. Those who had taken the plague with them or died of want, were buried in humble graves somewhere in the countryside. And with a keen sparkling frost and falling snow, those who had travelled further afield, adjudged it safe to return now. So it was that they arrived back by turns – on foot or horseback, in carts and waggons, in the swing of a coach – some chattering, some laughing, some grieving for family lost, and the streets of London Town regained something of their old vitality as, by and by, street callers gradually came out to sell their wares…

'What d' ye lack? What d' ye lack!'

'Oranges, oranges, fresh juicy oranges!'

'Good morrow, doctor, 'tis good to see the streets alive with people once more.'

'Ay, James, but 'tis sad. The last time I did hear the cry of *oranges*, the children played a game of catch. I played it with them – before they caught the plague. They were but little children, James.'

'Blessed children! I am yet benumbed by what befell, and yet methinks I have almost become a new man.'

'Ye have, indeed, James.'

'The lady Jessica hath shone where I was dull and pious. To see her take up her skirts and kneel amongst the filth and grime to scrub the floors and mop the ailing brow of distemper – though she was sick with the evil stench of their foetid breath – made me ashamed to be a priest. I shall marry her, doctor. If she will have me, I shall marry the lady Jessica.'

'Ay, James – I pray that she will have thee. See, more do return,' interrupted the doctor.

Horses neighed suddenly as a coach rattled in from the highway, and were reined in at the top of the square to set down a small group of travellers and their luggage. Among them, Samuel and Mopsa – weary, with a few poor belongings and a little dog yapping at their heels.

'Look who approaches,' said James. 'The seamstress and the shoemaker's 'prentice have returned. God be praised they have survived!'

'See, the ugly fug in the air hath gone, Mopsa,' said Samuel, looking about him.

'Ay, and the wintry sky is clear,' she said, 'yet what a strange feeling 'tis to be back, for all is so quiet.' She bent down and gathered up the little dog. 'I do think he should be safe now…'

'Ay, he should be safe,' said Samuel, 'but 'tis best to keep him hidden for a while.'

'Come,' she said, secreting the dog in her basket and covering it with a cloth. She stood there at the parting of the ways, for they had lived as little more than friends since leaving London in the early summer.

For the first two days after they left plague-struck London, Samuel and Mopsa had camped in a forest on the outskirts of the town, but the forest was heaving with unfortunate victims who believed they had been followed there by the avenging vapours. Misery had crouched under the bushes, beside the boles of trees, by the tracks leading back to the road, and it is hard to imagine the filth and rubbish that the multitudes had left in their wake.

The pair had gone on their way, taking the road to Norfolk pushing a hand-cart of dwindling provisions, and a little dog running by their side. Once they had put some distance between London and themselves, for fear of alienating local villagers wary of the distemper, they left their cart beside a track. Samuel carrying his shoemaking tools, including his last, and Mopsa with a bundle of clothes and the vestige of food they had left, had hitch-hiked along the way – flagging down hay carts and waggons until they arrived exhausted at his uncle's forge.

They had to work to earn their keep. Neither minded this, but separate tasks and the keen eye of an aunt had kept them apart. Now, like many who had been at sea and had been washed up onto an unfamiliar shore, Mopsa was virtually homeless unless she could find a suitable position with a chance to live in. She was one of many hundreds of citizens returning who had little or nothing to return to. The economic bubble that was London Town had burst, and many of the poor who had survived returned destitute seeking alms. Perhaps she could find work in a wealthy household or tailor's shop. She had been full of romantic notions about setting foot in London again, but Mopsa didn't wake up to the reality of her situation until she touched down from the coach and saw it rattle away…

'What intend ye now, Mopsa?' asked Samuel – with a glint in his eye.

'I did think…'

'I have the key to my uncle's shoemaker's shop, for it doth belong to me now.'

'Ay, I am glad for thee, Samuel.'

'Where will ye live now that we are back?'

'I did hope…' There was disappointment in her inflection, and she was just about to part with him when two poor brothers came and stood nearby.

'I could die for a crust,' said one.

'And I,' said the other.

Sensitive to their needs and his own, Samuel approached them. 'Good morrow, boy. Would ye work hard and learn how to soften neat's leather?'

'Ay,' said the boy, eagerly.

Samuel handed him a large key, and pointing said: 'Unlock that cobbler shop across the way if ye would be my 'prentice. And your friend…'

'My big brother,' cut in the boy.

Samuel approached his brother and said: 'You, fellow – There are pairs of boots and shoes looking for pairs of feet. Are ye willing to wear out thy boots and peddle mine?'

'Would that I had some good boots,' said the boy.

'Soon remedied, for ye shall have boots if ye would be my journeyman – selling boots and shoes and slippers for all.'

'Ay, sir!' said the boy, and bounded with his brother across the street to the cobbler shop.

'Well, Mopsa…' said Samuel.

She hung her head.

'It hath been good to know ye,' he said.

'Ay.'

He noticed the glint of a tear in her eye. 'Before ye go – I do need someone to sew my shirts – if they should be torn,' he teased.

'Thou impudent pig!' she cried, kicking and punching him – while the little dog yapped at his heels, attracting James to the rumpus.

'Unhand the gentleman,' he said.

'I shall not be unhanded!' said Samuel, and saw a change had come upon the priest.

'Ye are welcome back to London, both,' said James, 'and God be praised that ye are safe. What intend ye now?'

'I intend to marry Mopsa,' said Samuel.

'If I do agree,' she said.

'Then if ye condescend,' said James, 'accompany him to my church on the morrow, and I shall make arrangements for a wedding and publish the banns. I bid ye farewell.'

Samuel turned to Mopsa: 'What now, my love?'

'I shall tell ye by and by,' she said carelessly.

'Well, tell my by the morrow, not by and by. I have no time to parley, for I have a shoemaker's shop to open and two boys – down-at-heel – waiting for a job.'

'Ay.'

'Ay?'

'Ay, I shall marry thee,' she said.

James smiled. 'I shall see thee on the morrow!' He was on his way to the church when the doctor hailed him.

'I did forget, James. Today is the lady Jessica's birthday, and she is of age. Together, we are invited to her house to celebrate...'

'To the lady Jessica's house? She is of age?'

'Ay, I shall go thither at seven-of-the-clock, after I have been on my visits,' said the doctor. 'Will ye come?'

'I will,' said James. Farewell till then.'

As he passed by Jessica's garden gate, something remarkable caught James's eye, and he had to look twice to believe it at all. It was a winter rose with its petals open in half-bloom! All else were hips and dead leaves. It was the skeletal nature of the bush that had revealed the lonely flower. Scratching and pricking his fingers, he at last prised it from its bough. He held it up to the light, and could have sworn he saw the pink rose glitter in the manner of the early morning frost against the cobbles. He stood in awe, for it seemed as though he was looking at a flower picked from the fields of Heaven. The rose seemed to represent a great truth, in contrast to the filth and muck in the death-bound streets. 'This is hers,' he whispered, and went on his way, carefully guarding the rose.

32

Jessica, swathed in a thick woollen cloak, came back from the busy post-house with a letter from Huntingdon and opened it by the side of a roaring fire. Her parents, who had been overwhelmed with gladness at her survival, would be arriving late the following week. They had asked her to ensure certain provisions, and in that she engaged Thomas's help. There was no question of them objecting to Thomas or Mary who had both filled necessary positions well, but now she must search for a cook. For Jacob, Jessica was certain that he had a career as a chorister ahead of him – perhaps at the Chapel Royal – and intended to enlist James to the purpose.

She arrived back as five o'clock struck, and asked Thomas to bring in logs from the store and light another large fire in the dining room. 'Ye are all invited, for this is a special occasion. One-and-twenty – I can scarce believe it! I must do something with my hair – 'tis rats' tails,' she said, and hurried about the house to prepare for the party.

'I hope ye are well enough to join us, Mary.'

'I am a little better, madam.'

'Then ye shall play cards with Jacob tonight. I shall find thee clean clothes from the linen chest. When I am ready, I shall invite Thomas and little Jacob to sup with us.'

Jessica had spent many weeks in humble attire – suitable for the job of nurse-keeper, and it seemed strange to emerge in a flounce of blue silk, hair coiffed in fashion. Earlier, Thomas had brought bottles of sack wine from the cellar, while she had laid the table with heavy platters of bread, cheese and apple pie. It was the only dish she could make. She wanted the evening to be perfect and longed for James to appear, but the doctor arrived unaccompanied by James, and she was forced to veil her disappointment as they all gathered around the fire – eating and drinking and being merry, toasting her coming of age. It struck eight o'clock, and still James hadn't arrived.

'I shall light some more candles,' she said, swirling about the room with a taper. 'I wonder where the priest is?'

'We did meet earlier, and he did intend to come hither,' answered the doctor.

'Yet he hath not,' said Jessica.

James had been about to leave the church and make his way to Jessica's house when, suddenly, a distressed parishioner ran into the aisle distracted.

'I am the only one left of my family, sir. I cannot bear to live…'

'Nay, said James, do not say it…'

'I tell ye, priest, my life is lost.'

'Nay!'

'Thy sermon spoke of freedom. Ye said the plague was over, that God's vengeance did be spent, but 'tis not so. He hath taken my wife and child but yesternight. Wherefore? I ask ye, priest, wherefore?'

'I do be sorry – I cannot explain. Perchance the vapours lurked still within thy house or on thy clothes…'

Suddenly, the grieving parishioner drew a dagger

from its sheath and cried: 'I shall jump from the tower and leave this miserable life that hath no place for those I love.'

'Put down thy weapon, for I would speak to ye,' said James. 'So many have lost their lives or those they loved. Come let me pray with thee...'

'With thy avenging angels? Is there no room in hell, that they do break out on earth? Come no further, priest, for I shall end it!' he warned, making towards the spiral steps of the tower.

'No!'

Suddenly, Jessica's words came to him and James had the dreadful vision of a tragic citizen shamed, borne into his church feet first and buried afterwards in unhallowed ground.

After a struggle with his conscience, he had decided to protest and stir the clergy to compassion. He would have the heinous practice abolished, but much of the London clergy had been dispersed and there was no recourse to debate. Now, he faced the possibility of the lowly spectacle being enacted in his church, he himself presiding over events. It was too horrible to contemplate, and he began a lengthy exhausting interchange which at last persuaded the poor man to relent. He dropped his weapon and sobbed.

James made arrangements on his behalf and, the parishioner feeling of worth where he had felt worthless, went on his way – agreeing to meet a group of friendly souls for mutual companionship the following day.

It was almost nine thirty when James knocked on the

door or Jessica's house clutching the rose, and Thomas let him in. He had been standing at the back of the room for a while before she looked up and saw him staring at her, but she ignored him and carried on.

'Perhaps I shall play the lute,' she said.

'Ay,' said little Jacob, 'play the lute, for we can sing.'

'What is this tune? I have some Venetian music, but 'tis not suitable to accompany a song... 'Ah – Greensleeves. Surely we all do know it.' She strummed a few bars. 'What say ye, Jacob?' She sang to help him along... 'Sing, Jacob, and I shall accompany thee.'

The doctor laughed merrily. 'A goodly air! Ah, 'tis the best evening I have spent for many months.' He rose from his chair. 'At last the priest comes hither!'

The priest had eyes only for Jessica. She stopped singing as he approached, and strummed her lute suddenly out of tune, leaving Jacob to sing alone.

'Ye are in good voice, Jacob,' she said, 'Is he not, Mary?'

'Ay, madam. I would sing with him,' said Mary.

'When ye are recovered – but ye are tired Mary, and Jacob is too young to play at this time of the night. I do hope that all of ye have enjoyed my birthday celebration.'

'After all the unhappy times we have endured, 'tis one evening to remember with gladness, and I see the young ones do agree,' said the doctor.

'I am glad,' said Jessica. 'My father and mother do return soon, and when they do, we shall have some goodly gatherings. For now, 'tis time for Mary to return to her bed and rest...'

'Ay, and for Jacob,' said Thomas.

The doctor endorsed a match between his friends, and watched carefully for the outcome as James tried to approach Jessica with the rose and declare his love for her. When at last Jessica lit more candles and led the frail girl to her bed, the doctor began to tut and shake his head. 'Too slow, too slow,' he said. 'Do ye bid another suitor sally forth and pinch her from under thy nose?'

'Hush!' said James as she reappeared.

'Oh, I feel suddenly uncommon tired,' said the doctor, and lay back to sleep.

'I shall go to her my friend,' said James. The doctor did not answer, and began to snore.

James followed her to the far side of the room and said clumsily: 'I did find a rose – and I did pick it for ye – and….' He had rehearsed it, yet now stood before her and blushed. The devil!

'A winter rose! It is very beautiful…'

'Ay, 'tis beautiful like thee…' (Confound his tongue!)

'The best of presents…'

'Ay, and I bethought me – that…' He paused, continuing to stumble at his words.

'What did ye bethink, James?'

At that moment, the doctor prevented the very event he had encouraged…

'Madam, Come quickly!'

'The matter, Thomas?'

'The doctor, 'tis the doctor!'

They hurried over to find the doctor stretched out on the couch – his face flushed, his mouth inclining to one side. Jessica had learned well from him, and at once felt his pulse.

'It bounds and bounds… I must untie his neckcloth,' she said urgently.

'He hath enjoyed too much wine,' said James, 'and will recover anon.'

'Nay, James, I do not think he will,' Jessica said slowly. She turned to the gardener: 'Thomas, I thank ye for thy help – but 'tis time to take Jacob and retire. Already Mary sleeps.'

'Ay, madam. I do be sorry that thy birthday should so soon come to an end.'

'Yet we do have much good to remember,' she said.

Jessica was left alone with James, and together they watched over the doctor.

'What ails him, Jessica?'

'I do be sad to say 'tis apoplexy.'

'Tell me – what is apoplexy?'

'A seizure – 'tis like a raging of the blood that stops in the alleys of the brain, or… Oh, James, I do not know all. I am not a physician, only the nurse,' and she held the doctor's poor limp hand.

'Perchance another glass of wine…'

'No!'

'There is not another physician in the parish,' said James.

'That I know too well,' said Jessica. 'I am the only one to nurse him…Oh, dear God!' The stertorous breathing, that had persisted throughout their conversation, suddenly came to a halt.

Jessica felt his pulse again, and shook him: 'Awaken,

doctor, awaken!' She turned to James: 'I could not save him – yet he is with God, therefore I should be glad,' she sobbed.

James took her in his arms. 'No-one had a greater friend,' he said, battling with tears.

'I would not have him in the dead-cart. There is scarce room for burial – Oh, to save him that!' cried Jessica.

'He hath no kin, for his betrothed and all his family did die of an earlier visitation, 'tis why he did persist to find a cure,' said James.

'I did not know. Oh, 'tis sad. I do remember – he did not hail from London Town.'

'Nay. I shall arrange for his interment without, beside his family plot, and I shall take the service. He who mopped the brows of the humble – though he risked distemper – shall not be buried here. On the morrow, early, I shall to the Lord Mayor to tell him what hath befallen. Perchance there is a physician from another parish can share the burden.'

'Ay, and I shall go to his house and do what I can to straighten his affairs. If I am able, I shall help the sick – although I am no better than a quack.'

'Nay, Jessica, they are the words of grief. The doctor knew ye were a goodly nurse, and did defend thy mind. Ye are a wonder, Jessica – and I do love thee.'

'And I, thee,' and she kissed him. 'I shall preserve the rose,' she said.

'I shall stay and pray for our good friend tonight,' said James, covering him. 'Now I say goodnight, for ye must preserve thy modesty. Surely ye know ye have my heart, Jessica.'

'Ay,' she said, turning to him in a flicker of candlelight – 'I have always known.'

33

Fleas do not like a harsh frost, so the plague numbers dwindled to nothing now. Slowly, the people of London Town picked themselves up, and citizens continued to arrive from far and wide to claim family businesses or property they had inherited or wanted to buy. Unfamiliar faces appeared in the shops, bulks and behind the market stalls. Yet, sad to relate, many of those returning remained insensitive to the horror that had been – satisfied that they, themselves, had escaped...

Three days after the doctor's death, Jessica, wearing a cap and a linen dress befitting her work, endeavoured to help to put his house in order, while James organised his affairs. She was sorting out dried herbs from the summer and storing them in jars, when the new maid announced a visitor. She looked up from her task to see an important-looking personage standing before her. 'What ails ye, she asked?'

'Ails me?'

'Ay.'

She saw that he was well-to-do, periwigged, and carrying a walking cane. He looked at her, steely eyed, beneath a bulging brow: 'I might ask ye the same,' he said.

'Sir,' she answered, 'I am but helping ...'

'Ye are no longer required,' he cut in, looking down his nose, 'unless ye would be retained as a servant.'

'Nay, sir. I am a nurse-keeper.'

'Then thy infamy hath gone before ye.'

'Infamy?'

'Murderer of the sick.'

'Sir, I am astounded at thy impudence. I am a lady and a good friend and helper to the late doctor of this parish.'

He took a pinch of snuff. 'The doctor is dead. Ye are no longer required.'

'I do not take instructions from a stranger who hath not the courtesy to tell me his name,' she said.

'Sir Philip Hawker of the Royal College of Physicians – claiming the practice in this parish.'

'Ah – Sir Philip Hawker who among his like did turn tail and run before the plague.'

'Awaiting this moment – for none is left to pick up the pieces but I,' he said arrogantly.

'But what of my work? I do put the doctor's house in order.'

'Ye do trespass, for 'tis no longer his house but mine, and I bid ye good morrow,' he said with a dismissive gesture and, looking around as a conqueror surveying a new domain, added: 'Some changes shall be made.'

While he was occupied poking about with his walking cane and inspecting the doctor's muddle, Jessica furtively picked up a roll of paper from the desk, that she knew was important to her friend, and put it in her basket.

'I shall leave ye, sir,' she said. Then, putting on her cloak, she turned at the door and added: 'Ye shall know more of this!' And leaving the odious physician behind, she made her way to the church.

It had begun to snow. By the time she reached Church

Lane it was falling rapidly and drifting across the fields. James wasn't in the church when she arrived, but a woman, who was arranging the altar, told her he was in the vicarage close by behind the church and pointed the way. Jessica trod carefully around the edge of the graveyard, trying desperately to find the vicarage through the heavy snowfall, but she could barely see and, after she turned the corner, lost her way. As she walked first this way then that, trying to get her bearings, she stumbled upon something and, pushing herself up, gasped in sudden horror. It was a body! She had stumbled upon a plague-pit replete with barely covered victims. She stifled a scream, for the one that had caused her to stumble stretched out its frozen hand from the earth as though to pull her down.

'Oh, dear Lord have mercy!' she cried, and continued to stumble about blindly, not knowing where she was going or how to get there. Suddenly she bumped into someone who bore her up before she fell. 'Jessica!'

'James!'

'I did see thee from the window. Why do ye wander abroad in the snow? Ye are frozen. Come in and warm thyself by the fire.'

'James, I did see...'

'Yes. Ye should not have ventured there. The sexton hath not finished his work, for the ground is frozen.'

'It was horrible.'

'Ay, it doth speak of desperate times. Forget it. Come in. Give me thy wet cloak and warm thyself by the fire – and drink this mulled ale I did prepare for myself. I did want to see thee so much, Jessica, but was arranging matters for the good doctor. I did intend to visit this even.'

'So too was I engaged on his behalf.' Jessica was shivering now, with the cold and the shock of what she had witnessed. 'I do thank thee, James, for I am frozen – and never while I nursed the sick saw I such a horrible sight.' She sat down beside him and drank until the warm ale and the fire put her at ease. 'I do not wish to intrude, James, for I know ye are busy at work – but I shall go mad.'

'The matter?'

'Sir Philip Hawker comes to claim the doctor's house.'

'Nay! When he is yet warm?'

'I can no more help the sick or finish my work and there is still so much to do – for I did try so hard to put his house in order.'

'Ay. The good doctor hath only just demised, and 'tis certain that the wretched man usurps his property betimes.' He took her hands in his to warm them.

'The doctor did leave a message for me to copy this document. I found it on his desk,' she said, removing it from her basket.

'Perchance it was something he did want ye to have. Untie the riband, Jessica.'

Jessica untied the ribbon and unrolled the document: 'A will!'

'That I did witness with Sir John a short while ago,' said James, 'although I know not his bequest.'

'Here is a letter – 'tis for me.' She read by the light of the fire, astonished, and looked up 'The good doctor hath left me his property! – I do not need it – that he knew. It shall be sold for alms.'

James listened carefully. 'Nay, read more…'

'He regrets that I may never be a physician – that I did know – but begs me to "continue to work with the doctor in the parish" and "teach some goodly souls how to nurse the sick with knowledge and compassion." He doth want his house to be a school for nurses, James!' She laughed in glee: 'Sir Philip Hawker shall hear of this on the morrow. But wait – for he doth scribble a message overleaf: He bids me marry you!' she exclaimed. 'I shall not be told.'

The doctor had delivered an awkward silence.

James swallowed hard. 'I did want to ask thee, Jessica, the other night when he did die,' he said at length. He took her hands in his again, but she unknitted them.

'He hath written in riddles.'

'How so?'

Jessica stood up at once and reached for her cloak.

'Nay, 'tis not yet dry,' said James. 'I beg ye stay and give me thy answer, for I do love thee with all my heart.'

'And I thee.'

'Then…?'

'How can I marry thee, James, when I have work to do? – Do ye ask me to be the wife of a priest that should be ruled?'

'Nay!'

'Do ye bid me to trot behind ye like a maid, swinging a hatbox?'

'Nay, never, Jessica!'

'Or bid me to smile at thy congregation and play the

lute?'

'Nay!'

'Ye neigh like a horse – without understanding.'

'Lady!'

'I'll none it!' She picked up her basket, swept her cloak around her shoulders and was gone, leaving James to pace up and down his study in dismay.

The following morning, very early, James left the church and, slipping his way down the icy lane, stopped to hold on to a paling by Jessica's garden. The rose bush was covered, and there was no sign of life at all beneath the snowfall. Suddenly he heard a sound – bright and tuneful – reminding him of the blackbird that had sung for him in the summer. As he thought this, a robin alighted on a post and continued to sing as though to purify the world. 'Ye have the wings and the song of an angel,' he said, and went on his way in good spirits. He believed he knew what he had to do to gain Jessica's favour and, clinging on to what he could until he reached the doctor's house, he knocked boldly on the door.

Hawker had retained the maid. 'He is not yet up, sir,' she said.

'I shall wait.'

'Ay, sir,' and she showed him in.

James sat down and looked around him. Already the doctor's desk had been cleared and the swinging skeleton moved across the room. James considered it impertinence to do it so soon after the good doctor's demise. He waited in grudging mood until the door came suddenly open to reveal the arrogant figure of Hawker.

James stood up. 'Good morrow, sir.'

'Good morrow to ye. Who are ye, and what is thy business so early in the day? I see ye are in health,' he said, looking down his nose.

'For my name – I am James Throgmorton, priest of this parish, and my business is serious, sir.'

'How serious?'

'Ye must vacate this property, sir, forthwith.'

Hawker laughed, long and loud. 'A parish priest kicks me out?'

'If ye would prefer to feel my boot, I do.'

Hawker's smile faded. 'I would ask ye to leave, sir – on the instant.'

'I will not, for the property doth not belong to ye. It doth belong to the Lady Jessica Fitzgibbon – who ye did so rudely dismiss.'

'What proof have ye?'

'The only proof I need. She hath inherited it in the physician's will and hath the document in proof.'

Hawker wavered.

'This property is not thine. Ye do purloin it, sir,' continued James.

Down from his high horse, Hawker mopped his brow uneasily. 'I did not steal it but wait to buy it for my premises. Ye may ask my lawyer of my intent.'

'The owner is not yet cold and ye do consult thy lawyer? Ye should be ashamed to call thyself a gentleman. I bid ye seek another property in another parish. I bid ye good morrow, sir.'

Sir Philip Hawker gathered his belonging and slunk out of the door, leaving James satisfied with his own ability to rout him, self-assured that he had done so for Jessica. He sat   at the doctor's desk to reflect on the events as Jessica arrived to challenge Hawker on her own behalf. The new maid let her in.

'James?'

'Dear lady...'

'Dear lady? Is that all that ye can say? I was expecting to see Sir Philip Hawker, and it is plain ye are not he.'

'Nay, I am not – for he hath gone.'

'Gone?'

'I did tell him of the will.'

'Ye did presume – Ye did presume to fight my battle?'

'I did but try to help.'

'Ye have not.'

'Have not?'

'Nay, ye did interfere, thinking my business was not mine own.'

'I did not mean...' Suddenly, he rose against her: 'I shall endure it no more. Ye ever see the worst in me, Jessica, and I shall no longer aby it. Believe me, I would have stood by thee in thy work – despite the social censure. I tried to tell ye, but ye would not incline thine ear. Now 'tis clear ye do not love me as I have loved thee.'

His words stunned her: 'But James...'

'I wish thee good morrow.' He turned and went from the door.

'...as I have loved thee.' She repeated the words that had stunned her – and before long she wept.

34

In springtime, after the distemper had taken its last life – for it had come back for another helping after the winter – the citizens of London Town were finally able to go about their business again in the knowledge that they had seen the last of the worst plague in their history. The Great Plague, as it came to be known, had claimed up to a hundred thousand lives. As they went about their business, the tragedy that had affected the lives of them all began to pass into collective memory, surfacing only as the nightmare of the past.

Despite her unconventional methods, Jessica had influenced James for the better. He had changed his idea of God, become more attuned to the gentler things in life, less moralistic, more tolerant of others, but he had offended she who had brought about this change by meddling in her affairs and defending himself. Since he had parted with her so bitterly, he had looked for her in vain: in his church, by the doctor's house, at the market, beside the rose bush that hung over her gate. It was clear she was avoiding him. But the truth was other than that. Jessica was busy absorbing herself in her studies and, if there was a need, would accompany the new parish doctor to assist him in his work.

Shortly after James had parted with her Jessica's parents returned, delighted to find their only child fit and well after the devastating plague. Yet their delight didn't last long, for it was with consternation that they learned about their daughter's nursing on the streets and in the hovels, and a bitter battle ensued.

'It is not meet for a young lady of thy birth to dress in the manner of a servant,' said her mother. 'I forbid ye to do it.'

'So too do I,' said her father, a passive soul who often chimed his wife.

'Was it meet for ye to leave me to an uncertain fate?' Jessica countered.

'It was thy decision...'

'Embraced by thee.'

'Ye would have spread it abroad.'

'I had naught to spread – but my goodwill, and for this I was saved.'

'The plague is over now and ye may let it rest,' said her mother.

'Nay, Mama, it blows like an ill seed that cares not where it lands, and I shall help to root it out.'

'Ye talk in riddles, girl.'

'I shall remind ye that I am of age and there is nothing ye can do to stop me.'

'But for thy inheritance...'

I care not. I have my work.'

'Work?'

'I say I care not.'

'Oh, give me my salts – I shall faint!'

James noticed Sir Andrew and Lady Fitzgibbon take a front pew in his church one Sunday morning, but was disappointed to note that Jessica's place was empty beside them. He concluded his lengthy sermon: '... and so I say to ye: Be not afraid to entertain strangers, for thereby some have entertained angels unaware.' His service came to an end with a rumble of approval from his newly-inflated congregation, and each member rose to thank him before leaving his church – but Jessica's parents lingered.

'Sit ye there,' her mother said, 'and rest thy kibes.'

'Ay,' said Sir Andrew, compliant.

She turned to James. 'Good morrow, Rev…?'

'James Throgmorton, Lady Fitzgibbon.'

'Ah, yes. I am glad to see ye well.'

'And I am glad to see ye returned safely, my lady.'

'Something of moment, sir,' she said conspiratorially. 'I have thy confidence?'

'As a man of the cloth.'

'I would speak with ye in private.'

'Without thy husband?'

'It should concern him not,' she said – with a peremptory wave of her fan.

James smiled wryly, and thought her a lady, who like her daughter, knew not the social order. 'Then please sit down,' he invited.

'We have not attended for a while, sir, therefore I do not know if ye know my daughter – the lady Jessica.'

His heart leapt.

'She is naughty girl,' said her mother.

'Nay – ye do surprise me.'

'Dost know that she hath been among the streets?'

'I have seen her – at times – but not of late,' he said honestly.

'She hath been absent from the house for nights and days. She doth study books, sir. What say ye to that?'

'I shall look for a text to refer to this, lady, but I do think there is none.'

'Then the Good Book is wanting, sir!'

'Is this the sum of thy complaint against thy daughter, my lady?'

'Nay. She doth follow the young doctor...'

He swallowed hard. 'The young doctor?'

'Ay, he that is new to the parish – and they do go about the streets to nurse the sick.'

The church spun around him, and he could have collapsed at the news so carelessly bestowed. He groped for words.

'The sick need tending, lady...'

'By a lady of high birth? Fie! I would have ye seek her out and counsel her, and gather her to thy flock.'

'If the lady Jessica is of age...'

'She is, sir.'

'Then there is naught to be done – although I acknowledge thy concern.'

'Naught to be done? I see ye have wasted my time,' said Lady Fitzgibbon and, collecting her husband from the pew, added: 'Good morrow, sir,' and left the church.

James tortured himself with visions of Jessica and her new love and, some while later to compound his anxiety, the handsome young physician approached him in the market place.

'Good morrow, sir. It is my good fortune to meet ye,' said the physician.

'Good morrow,' said James.

'I am Christopher Gilchrist, the new physician of this

parish, and do intend to come to thy church very soon.'

'Ye are welcome, sir,' said James, reeling.

'I thank thee. With the warmer weather we have been busy with a new – though little – outbreak of the plague.'

'I did hear.'

'Now 'tis over sir, I shall marry, and would ask ye to call the banns.'

'Marry?'

'Is it not usual, sir?'

'Ay, nay...'

'I shall be with ye with my betrothed – What say ye – Sunday after evensong?'

The room continued to spin.

'Sunday, after evensong?' Repeated James distractedly.

'Sir? – Shall we see ye then, sir?' persisted the new doctor.

'Ay,' said James, lost for his own name.

'I am glad, for I would marry her! Good morrow, priest.'

Jessica to be married, though she was once to be his! He could have wept, and tortured himself until Sunday came. But he had tortured himself in vain, for he saw neither the young doctor nor Jessica at Evensong, but shortly after the service, when the congregation had gone home, he saw the young doctor hurrying though the lynch-gate with a young woman. It was not Jessica, but the doctor's betrothed. Her name was Anne.

James had imagined what he feared most, and had been tortured by the sort of misconception that is often planted and left to flourish in the minds of lovers. Could it be that Jessica was still his? Yet he dared not approach her for fear of being spurned.

For Jessica, she dared not hope that he still loved her, and was too proud to plead with him. Meanwhile, she immersed herself in her studies, and contemplated a new beginning – a little school for nurses.

35

It was early July. London was alive, and the town crier paraded the square, ringing a happier bell. Stalls and bulks, replete with goods, heaved with custom and more street- sellers gathered to call their wares. The surviving children came out to play, kicking their pig's bladder ball about the square, a sight – one of many – that reminded James of his first encounter with Jessica.

On occasions, he had caught sight of her in the market place or making her way down Church Lane, but he had hung back. So often he'd wanted to call at her home or at the doctor's house, but the more time went by the more awkward he felt, and there was something else. As relieved as he was that the plague had ended, the whole ethos of London seemed to change with the situation – drawing them further apart. Jessica felt it too.

She had seen the pompous Archdeacon and the Bishop, each of whom had fled in fear the previous year, visit the church lately – no doubt to take stock of parochial business, and she resented them on James's behalf. (In truth, now that the plague was over, and despite his young age, they were magnanimously considering him for the post of Vicar).

As for the household, Jessica felt alienated now that her parents had returned. When she was not attending to her work with the physician, she could be found in her room at her studies or seeking the company of Thomas and little Jacob who would soon be joining the Chapel Royal choir school.

'I am so proud of ye, Jacob, for now ye shall sing for

the King!'

'I did say he could come back to see us – and the cat – for this is his family now,' said Thomas.

'Ay, we are his family now,' agreed Jessica.

'The roses bloom well this year, madam,' said Thomas.

'They are lovely.'

But there was no vitality in her reply, and she returned to her room. She opened the flower press to see the winter rose looking back at her, preserved from months before. She longed to recapture the moment he had given it to her – yet she had argued with him, teased him, disdained him! Her reverie ended when Mary knocked on her door.

'What is it, Mary?'

'Thy mother asks for thee.'

Lady Fitzgibbon was busying herself – patting about – when Jessica approached. 'Thy cousin Juliet is to be married – and to a baronet!' said her mother.

'Oh, I am pleased for her...'

'We are invited...'

'I do not wish...'

'Ye do not wish? Cousin Juliet hath ever been a friend to ye. Ye cannot choose but go...'

'Ye are right, Mama. I do forget myself. Cousin Juliet hath been as a sister to me. There are few sick and the doctor doth not need me a while.'

'What a mercy,' said her mother sarcastically.

Jessica ignored the comment. It was one of many. 'When shall we go?'

'The day after the morrow – and ye shall take thy

maid, Mary. Ye shall have thy gown fashioned on the estate. We go for a month.'

Moments later, James came by her gate on his way to the market place, and noticed the roses in full bloom crowding over the wall but, painfully reminded of Jessica, he continued to the market place. There, he came across Mopsa buying asparagus from the street-seller.

'Good morrow, Mopsa.'

'Good morrow, priest.'

'Ye are, I trust, well?'

'Ay, sir – for we do move away from London on the morrow.'

'How so?'

'The shop be too small for a family,' she said, tapping her belly, 'and the two boys that do work for us – and the dog. We do move – all of us – to a bigger shop in Norfolk.'

'Then I wish ye well, and God bless ye, Mopsa.'

'Fare thee well, sir.'

At that moment in the square, James had considered his own life, for it had become dull. His sermons were uninspired; he found meetings with the Bishop and the Archdeacon tedious; he had no will to listen to the gossip of his congregation; the churchwarden irritated him and, reflecting on his negative feelings, he accused himself of sheer misanthropy. The truth was simpler than that. He missed Jessica, for though she had argued with him constantly, she had been the piquant sauce so long missing in his life, but with each day that went by, it had become more difficult for him to make amends. Little did he know that Jessica, in her own ennui, had resolved to try to put an end to their estrangement as soon as she returned to London. But their reunion was not to be as simple as she supposed – courtesy of a baker in Pudding Lane – for on the second day of August, very early in the morning before anyone was up, London began to burn…

36

Flames consumed the church doors and entered like an enemy, whooshing along the aisle and up the tower in rising columns thick with smoke. On sprang the flames in every direction, leaping the thatches of inns and hovels; across to the market place it raged, licking hungrily, gorging itself on stalls, bulks, barrels and boxes of goods – greedy for anything in its van.

As the flames climbed up the inn, the ostler let the horses from their stables and they galloped wildly whinnying and neighing instinctively towards the Thames. Others, saddled but rider-less, bounding madly in the same direction, made for the river and swam. Horses and citizens, together, bobbed and floated in the water and boats could take no more. Leather buckets – no weapon against the hungry flames – were filled and re-filled as chains of the able-bodied passed them along with shouts and shrieks of defeat, but the water was flung in vain. The fire would not be sated …

'Fire! Fire!' In the early morning, James had awoken to a loud banging on his door and the cries of the churchwarden. Choking, he opened up to see the sexton and the grave-diggers filling buckets from the water pump to douse the flames; the fire had spread while they slept and their efforts were as nothing against the blaze that surrounded them, already rising in columns fed by wood and wind.

James pulled on shirt, breeches and boots and, though not the brawny sort, rolled up his sleeves. He tried with all his might to help but his efforts were in vain, for the more he tried, the more the fire raged. In the midst of the commotion – for more souls had appeared to offer help – he suddenly cried out: 'Jessica!' – enough to startle the heavens, and hurried through the lynch-gate – already licked with flames – to her garden.

Palisade, outhouse, all began to flame. He circumvented the fire, kicked the back door in and entered the house still calling madly for Jessica; the fire had already entered from the front and was doing its worst. Beams, furniture, wall-hangings, all flaming in black smoke, and the oak stairway was engulfed in the blaze. He hurried from the house, and to his horror came upon the bodies of the cook and the gardener, who had died overcome by the toxic fumes as he ran to her aid. He ran towards the lane but turned back in a last hope of finding Jessica. He entered the brick shed which was just repelling the flames. Jessica was not there, but crouching in the corner, behind a lethal pile of wooden boxes and sacks, was a little boy cuddling a cat, his eyes wide with terror.

'Jacob?'

Jacob was too terrified to speak.

'I want ye to follow me,' said James at once.

Jacob clutched the cat, protectively.

'Take my hand, Jacob.' James realised that the little boy was afraid for the cat, and   still refused to move so, quickly emptying a sack of potatoes, he said urgently.

'Put thy cat in the sack.'

But Jacob responded warily.

'Save thy cat!'

Jacob suddenly sprang up, put the cat in the sack,

clutched it to him and together they hurried from the garden and into the field across the lane. The hovel was ablaze and the wheat caught on fire. James looked this way and that, afraid they would be trapped. In the most tender moment of his spiritual life, he felt more sorrow for the little boy who stood there – so trustingly clutching his cat – than for himself. As he began to pray, there came a whinny in answer: a horse in need of a rider stood before him. He secured the cat, got up onto the horse and, taking Jacob with him, galloped he knew not where...

For Jessica, it was a long, rough journey back to London by coach and, as they neared London Town, they saw a distinct glow ahead of them.

'What is the light over London, for it is long past dawn?' she asked.

'Flames, madam,' said Mary.

'Nay it cannot be,' said Jessica.

The horses whinnied in warning and, a little further along the way, became ungovernable. The coachman reined them in and came to a sudden halt on the highway. He got down and looked in at the coach window 'London is burning, sir! Look! London's afire!'

'Ye do mistake,' said Lady Fitzgibbon.'

'The horses will go no further, my lady.'

'Go no further?'

'Do ye ask us to walk?' objected her husband, getting out of the coach to see for himself, and doing so shouted: 'Fire! London is on fire!'

'London is burning, my lady – look! London is on fire!'

cried Mary.

'Turn back along the track to yonder inn,' ordered Sir Andrew.

Jessica had been watching and listening in horror. 'Help me down,' she told the coachman.'

'Nay, ye shall not!' exclaimed her mother, thrusting out her hand.

'Then I shall help myself – for I cannot stand aside from this...'

Suddenly, one of the horses reared and emitted a dreadful shriek and, in the moment before the coach turned, Jessica jumped down and watched it lurch clumsily back along the track.

She found herself lying on the highway – just before the market square where the coaches were accustomed to stop, and where a gaggle of geese and other livestock had now taken refuge. She got up and hurried to the market where some flames still lingered and most fixtures were reduced to charcoal. The fire had been burning for three days. Some flames flickered, while other conflagrations had started elsewhere – in a hayloft, in a thatch, in the cooper's yard, lighting the barrels... Wisps of smoke came from smouldering wood at her feet as she picked her way around it. The alleyways were no more, for the close houses that fashioned them were now heaps of charred timber and ash, and the doctor's house – for she still called it that – was gone. It was a ghost town of the most horrible sort, for all the people had fled.

Jessica shed no tears. They wanted to come, but could not. She made her way carefully to Church Lane, terrified of what she might see, and started to run, directionless, for she could not find her house at first. Then, prompted by instinct, it stood before her – a burnt-out shell of smouldering devastation.

'No!' she cried. 'Jacob! Thomas!'... She called in vain. Terrified, she fled from the house to the church. The lynch-gate had burned down, and she continued through a shell. The heavy oak doors of the church had been consumed, and inside she could see that the pews were turned to ashes and still smouldered, the altar had fallen and the walls crumbled. 'Oh, God! God!' She ran back. The church tower rocked, for the fire had consumed the mortar, and bricks began to tumble down. 'James! James!' she cried and ran for safety into the field by the lane.

Exhausted, insensible, Jessica looked around and, through the smoke that hung in the air – for the grass and ricks had been ablaze, she vaguely discerned a figure waving at her through the smoke: 'James!' she called. It was not James but Christopher Gilchrist the physician. He came closer, out of breath.

'What in God's name, hath happened?' she breathed.

'The best part of London hath gone up in smoke – except Westminster that it did circumvent. Some killed, some crowd the river...'

'I thank God that ye were saved. Where is Anne?'

'People were mounting the riderless horses that galloped into the field. There were not enough for all, but a goodly soul did haul her up and take her with him.'

'Whither?'

'To Moorfields – where multitudes take refuge. For

myself, I dove into the ditch and was saved, for the flames were consuming the very ground.'

'I must to Moorfields – with but a little hope of finding the man I love.'

'I shall gladly go with ye. I have my bag, for there will be many citizens in need of physic. I beg ye to assist me.'

'I shall. How far to Moorfields?'

'Not two miles north of here.'

'Then let us hasten thither.'

Two days earlier, James had followed others – some on horseback, some trudging on foot – making their way to Moorfields. It was a pitiful sight. Hundreds of people, of diverse needs, gathered exhausted in the fields without food or belongings. Many of them sat on the grass in bewilderment unable to utter a word, while others whimpered and cried out. Who would have believed that London Town could have been dealt such a tragedy less than a year after the plague had ended?

James left Jacob in the care of a friendly woman while he went about the people leading prayers. Some citizens were grateful to him, but many of them railed against God and sought answers, but it consoled him that Jacob was in good hands. The woman had at once covered him with her shawl and taken charge of the cat, while James attempted to appease some of the distressed members of his unwieldy congregation.

Now, in London Town, the King rode into his finest hour with the Duke of York, actively trying to douse the flames and, galloping ahead, ordered the pulling down of dwellings in the path of the fire. At the same time, he gave orders for sustenance to be sent to Moorfields from the military stores, together with tents courtesy of the Navy. Now, like the King, citizens from Westminster and outer London were prompted to send what help they could.

Little Jacob continued to be anxious for his cat, but the next day, benevolent dairy farmers loaded a cart with milk and sent it post haste to Moorfields. Jacob and the cat drank.

Two days later, Jessica and the physician arrived by foot to help. Overwhelmed by casualties with burns and other injuries, they did what they could for the people and at last Jessica lay down on the grass exhausted. 'God knows when we shall meet again,' said the physician, and parted with her to look for Anne.

As Jessica lay there, her eyes at last began to fill with tears. She was exhausted and had reached her nadir. Suddenly, from somewhere among a whimpering crowd, she heard angelic notes floating easily on the air. Someone was singing! She sat up and listened. It came from close by. She got up and traced the sound. 'Jacob!' she cried. He ran to her clutching his cat, and suddenly pointed and cried out: 'And the priest comes!'

The priest was walking towards her wearing a filthy shirt with his sleeves rolled up, his face covered in dirt and smuts...'James! Oh, James!' she cried. He looked up: 'Jessica!' She ran to him as fast as her weary legs would carry her and sank in his arms.

Together with Jacob and his cat, they travelled north by coach to the uncle's estate. Had they ventured back to St. Bride's, all that they had known would be a barren wasteland, tinged with the deep sadness of memory. No longer was the church standing at the top of the lane that led down to the market square; no longer did the musk roses hang over the gate by the wall. The streets, lanes and alleyways, once so busy with life joyful and tragic, were no more. All that was familiar in London Town – including all traces of the plague – had gone to rest forever in the dust.

THE END

www.blossomspringpublishing.com